Sugar and Spice

AN L.A. CANDY NOVEL

BOOKS BY LAUREN CONRAD

L.A. Candy

Sweet Little Lies
AN L.A. CANDY NOVEL

LAUREN CONRAD
Style

LAUREN CONRAD

Sugar and Spice

AN L.A. CANDY NOVEL

HARPER

An Imprint of HarperCollins*Publishers*

This book is dedicated to Maura, Lo, Jillian, Natania, and Britton because they have always been there for me. I am honored to call them my very best friends.

Library of Congress Cataloging-in-Publication Data is available.
ISBN 978-0-06-176762-3 (trade bdg.)
ISBN 978-0-06-201148-0 (int. edition)

Typography by Andrea Vandergrift
10 11 12 13 14   CG/BV   10 9 8 7 6 5 4 3 2 1

First Edition

D-LISH

(GOSSIP YOU HATE TO LOVE)

Things are getting sticky on the set of *L.A. Candy*: Our girl-next-door Jane Roberts has survived a tabloid scandal and somehow managed to come back sweeter than ever. But the good life has soured for ex-BFF Madison, who has been outed as a calculating schemer. Meanwhile, Scarlett, that tart-tongued beauty, is keeping the rumor mill busy with whispers of a secret boyfriend. . . .

With Season 2 around the corner, who knows what drama these tasty starlets will cook up next!

1

NOT DATING

"Over here!"

"Let's get a shot of the two of you!"

"Smile, girls!"

Jane Roberts felt hands on her shoulders—her publicist? random PopTV assistants?—maneuver her into place as several paparazzi shouted out to her and Scarlett Harp. Nearby, dozens of fans waved wildly, screamed the girls' names, and snapped photos with their cell phones.

Scarlett bent her head toward Jane's. "What are the rules on skipping the red carpet at your own premiere?"

"Ha-ha," Jane said, grinning. "Think you're gonna have a hard time getting out of this one, Scar."

"I'm giving them five minutes, then heading inside for a drink. Something tells me I'm gonna need it tonight."

"Good luck. I think we're stuck here till, like, seven thirty. Besides, live television and booze aren't the best combination. And I'm pretty sure the two drinks you had at dinner should tide you over."

Scarlett rolled her eyes. "Whatever."

Flashbulbs began popping brightly. Jane took a deep breath, fixed a smile on her face, and tried not to feel overwhelmed. Of course PopTV made sure the media was out in full force on the red carpet for *L.A. Candy*'s Season 2 premiere. Their little show had somehow become the top rated on the network, and a lot was riding on the premiere. The party would air live on PopTV, to be immediately followed by the episode itself.

Jane glanced over her shoulder at the sprawling lawn of the magnificent Spanish-style Hollywood Hills mansion. Hundreds of people were at this event: photographers, fans, and an assortment of entertainment industry types. On a makeshift stage near the infinity pool, pop star Aja was revving up to sing. There were TV cameras everywhere.

PopTV really knew how to throw a party!

"Scarlett, turn more to the left," a photographer shouted.

"Stand closer together!" another one added.

Jane obeyed, never breaking her smile. After all, as one of the four main girls on *L.A. Candy*, tonight was work, not play (even though she had to *act* as though she was having fun).

But Scarlett wasn't quite so understanding. "Good thing they're here to tell me how to pose for a picture. I couldn't have figured it out without them," she muttered. She glared at a PopTV assistant who was coming toward her with a powder brush; the assistant backed off.

"Scar!" Jane whispered.

"Yeah, yeah, I know. I'm trying my best."

As the photographers continued shouting directions and taking pictures—why was it taking soooo long?—Jane kept her smile in place and resisted the impulse to touch her long, blond, wavy hair, which felt stiff and weird from the insane amount of hair spray the PopTV stylists had subjected it to. Nor was she totally comfortable in her black ruffle dress by a new designer named Mario Nuñez, which accentuated her five-foot-five, sort-of-in-shape figure nicely, but made her feel way older than her nineteen years. Nuñez's publicist had worked it out with Jane's publicist: a free dress for Jane in exchange for publicity for Nuñez. (Jane could see the magazine caption now: "Jane Roberts rocks a Nuñez strapless at the *L.A. Candy* premiere!")

Before famed producer Trevor Lord chose her to be on his new reality TV show, Jane had no idea that so many "spontaneous" celebrity photos ("Anna Payne stocks up on pumpkin soap at Lush!" "Jared Walsh hand-feeds sushi to Brazilian supermodel Catarina at Geisha House!") were actually prearranged by publicists. Of course, before *L.A. Candy*, Jane had been clueless about what really went on in Hollywood. Now that *she* was a celebrity (although she still had a hard time thinking of herself that way), her life had completely changed. She and Scar were no longer the anonymous girls from Santa Barbara who moved to L.A. seven months ago, Jane to intern with a top event planner, and Scar to be a freshman at USC. Back then, the girls didn't wear nine-hundred-dollar designer dresses that they didn't have to pay for, and paparazzi didn't try to record their every move.

"Gaby! Let's get you in the picture, honey!" one of the publicists called out.

Gaby Garcia, the third *L.A. Candy* girl, waved to the photographers as she walked up to Jane and Scarlett. "Hey, have you been inside yet? There are soooo many hot guys here!" she gushed.

"Hey, Gaby," Jane said. She liked Gaby, who could be a little spacey but was sweet and easy to hang out with. She looked pretty tonight in a pale mocha sequined slip dress.

Scarlett wrapped an arm around Gaby's shoulders. The two of them had become fast friends in the last few months, which Jane thought was kind of funny, because they couldn't be more different. "Hey, stranger. What's new?"

"Not much. Oh, yeah, I got highlights!" Gaby patted her light brown updo and peered around. "Where's Madison? Shouldn't she be in the picture, too?"

Madison. Jane pretended to adjust her dress in an attempt to mask her reaction to Gaby's comment. She couldn't let the photographers—or anyone else—see her lose her cool. If she and Gaby and Scarlett were going to discuss Madison at all, it was better to do so "backstage" behind a locked bathroom door, not on the red carpet where every word and facial expression was being noted, recorded, scrutinized.

The fourth girl on the show, Madison Parker, was the last person Jane wanted to see tonight—or ever (although of course she was *here*, somewhere, so an encounter was inevitable). Three months ago, just before Christmas, Madison secretly leaked photos of Jane hooking up with her then-boyfriend Jesse's best friend, Braden. When the story broke in *Gossip* magazine, Jane almost had a breakdown, and Madison pretended to be a good friend and came to her rescue, holding her hand through the entire painful, humiliating ordeal. Madison even let Jane move into her penthouse apartment after Jane and Scar had a big fight.

After she found out what Madison had done, Jane packed her bags and moved back in with Scar, full of apologies. That was on Valentine's Day, five weeks ago, and Jane and Madison hadn't spoken since. Jane had told Trevor in no uncertain terms that she would not film any scenes with Madison ever again. She still couldn't believe she had fallen for Madison's act, or that she had chosen a backstabber like Madison over Scar, who had been her best friend since kindergarten.

Scarlett squeezed Jane's hand and turned to Gaby. "Madison's probably getting an emergency Botox treatment," she said, too low for anyone else to hear. "I guess her mom never told her that being a manipulative, lying bitch can cause wrinkles."

"Funny," Gaby said, giggling awkwardly. She was

obviously uncomfortable poking fun at Madison. Gaby and Madison were close, or they used to be, anyway. Jane wasn't sure where things stood between them these days. Jane wondered if Gaby felt weird being friends with Madison, even though Madison hadn't done anything to her personally, because Gaby was friends with Jane and Scarlett, too, and maybe she was worried about seeming disloyal to one or the other side?

Out of the corner of her eye, Jane saw Dana, one of the PopTV producers, hurrying across the lawn toward them, clipboard in hand. The woman looked super-stressed, as usual. And she was dressed in all black again, except her outfit was more tailored and less faded than her standard attire. She had even put on makeup, which was saying a lot, considering that the most Jane had ever seen on her face were the remains of her morning muffin.

"Okay, everyone, thanks, but I need to talk to the girls," Dana said loudly, ushering Jane, Scarlett, and Gaby toward the end of the press line and off the red carpet. "Listen up, ladies. In"—she squinted at her watch—"ten minutes, Alli's going to take you over to the back terrace so you can get miked for the intro segment kicking off the party. There will be people to touch up your hair and makeup. As soon as we're done shooting that, we'll move you over to the statue garden for a segment leading into the first commercial break. And then . . . let's see . . . Jane, I'm going to need you to do another segment, to introduce

Aja. Everyone's lines will be up on the teleprompters, so don't worry about that."

"Why can't *I* introduce Aja? She's, like, my favorite singer ever!" Gaby complained.

"That's fine with me," Jane offered.

Dana gave Gaby an impatient look. Gaby pouted and mumbled, "Okay, whateverrrrr."

"Ten minutes, all right?" Dana reminded them. "Alli will . . . *What*, Ramon?" she barked into her headset. "What do you *mean* Hannah's got the flu? Well, is she throwing up? We need her to—" Dana hurried away. Hannah Stratton, who worked with Jane at Fiona Chen Events, was on the show from time to time. She and Jane were good friends, on and off camera. Jane hoped she was okay.

"Sorry about Aja," Jane apologized to Gaby, who simply shrugged and snatched a glass of champagne off someone's tray.

Jane felt bad (especially since she was pretty sure that it was another guest's partially consumed champagne Gaby had just taken from a busboy, not a waiter). Jane wished that Dana and Trevor wouldn't treat her as the star of *L.A. Candy*, since the show was supposed to be about the everyday lives of all four girls, equally. In the beginning, Dana had explained to Jane that viewers seemed to relate to her the most. But why? Okay, so maybe Scar intimidated people by being so beautiful (without even trying)

7

and rocket-scientist smart. And maybe Madison used way too much makeup and hair bleach for the average viewer. What about Gaby, though? Why wasn't *she* relatable? She was nice, funny, cute, and had a cool job at a PR firm called Ruby Slipper.

"Oh, I almost forgot to tell you guys!" Gaby said suddenly. She handed her empty champagne glass to a random party guest, who glared at her, and fished through her black beaded clutch. "Here," she said, holding out a business card. "This woman came up to me before. She said she's a publicist, and she wants to talk about repping me."

Scarlett took the card from Gaby, and she and Jane studied it. It read, ANNABELLE WEISS, followed by an address on La Cienega Boulevard and some other contact info.

"She sounds—" Jane began.

"Sketchy," Scarlett finished.

Jane made a face. "Scar! I was about to say *great*. I love, love, love my publicist! Gaby, you should have one, too. So should you, Scar."

"Why, so I can get into more trashy tabloids, talking about my cayenne-pepper-and-celery-juice diet?" Scarlett said.

"You mean your Chinese-takeout-and-pizza diet?" Jane teased her. "Seriously, Sam totally turned my image around after . . . you know . . ." She hesitated, not wanting to say the words "*Gossip* scandal" out loud. The subject still pained her. "She got a lot of really good articles about me in the magazines," she went on. "And she, uh, talked to all the reporters about me and Jesse so I didn't have to." Actually, she didn't feel much like saying the word "Jesse" out loud, either.

"You mean when he started getting wasted all the time and hooking up with other girls?" Gaby said. Gaby was like that—no filter. She wasn't trying to be mean; she just blurted out whatever she was thinking, without thinking.

Scarlett ignored Gaby's comment and motioned to Jane, indicating that she look behind her. Caleb! Her high school boyfriend had made it to the party.

"Come on, Garcia. Let's go check out the hors d'oeuvres," Scarlett said, shrugging and smiling at Jane as she led Gaby toward one of the catering tables.

"Janie!"

Jane found herself face-to-face with Caleb. She hadn't seen him in a few weeks, not since she found out that he'd recently moved to L.A. He was as gorgeous as ever, especially in his dark red button-down shirt and jeans.

"Caleb! I'm glad you could come! Is Naveen here?" Jane had also invited Naveen Singh, another high school classmate and Caleb's best friend.

"Naveen had to go to Boston for some family thing," Caleb said with a smile. "God, it's great to see you!"

Caleb started to give her a hug. Jane glanced around quickly, making sure they were alone. She didn't need photographers catching her having a mini-reunion with her ex. Or worse, Trevor or one of the other producers, who would surely seize on Caleb as a potential TV "love interest" for Jane. She and Caleb had split up almost a year ago, and in any case, she was taking a break from boys. She didn't need the drama after what she'd been through recently.

Since no one seemed to be paying attention, Jane let Caleb scoop her up in his arms, which felt unexpectedly warm and familiar. And strong—probably because he used to be on the swim team, and wasn't he working in construction these days?

"You look amazing in that dress," he whispered in her ear.

Jane blushed. "Thanks. I—"

Someone's cell began buzzing. It took Jane a second to realize that it was hers. She wriggled out of Caleb's embrace and peeked at the screen. BRADEN CALLING. *Ohmigod, Braden?* Why was he calling her? He'd emailed her a couple of times after her breakup with Jesse, to check in on her, but that had been it.

She and Braden had always been friends, and at the same time way more than friends, although the timing had never worked out for them to actually *date.* But why was her heart racing so fast at the thought of hearing his voice?

"I, uh, have to get this," Jane told Caleb. "I'll catch up with you later, okay?"

"No worries. I can just hang out here and wait," Caleb said.

Jane turned her back to him and hit Talk. "Hello?"

"Hey, Jane. It's Braden."

"Hey. Where are you?"

"Well, I'm sitting here flipping through channels and seeing your face. They're showing these commercials for your party tonight."

"You mean the 'teasers'?"

"Yeah, those. Sorry I couldn't make it, by the way. I just wanted to call and, you know, wish you luck. Not that you need it. You look great, Jane. I mean it."

"Aww, that's so sweet. Thanks!"

Jane had invited Braden as a courtesy, knowing he would never come. He hated the Hollywood scene and didn't want anything to do with *L.A. Candy*, refusing to sign a release to be on the show. Mostly, it was because being an aspiring actor and being on reality TV didn't mix. Jane also suspected that he wanted to stay out of the media spotlight as much as possible after the *Gossip* nightmare.

"Is that your mom?" Caleb asked Jane. "If it is, tell her I said hi!"

Jane glanced up, startled. She hadn't realized that Caleb was still standing there. Was this his immature way of trying to find out if it was a guy?

"Who was that?" Braden asked her.

"What? Oh, um, that's Caleb," Jane replied.

"Caleb? Who's Caleb?"

Awkward. "He's . . . um . . . an old friend."

"Hey! Who are you calling an old 'friend'?" Caleb teased her. "That one of your new boyfriends, Janie?"

"No!"

11

"No, what?" Braden said, sounding puzzled.

"I was just telling Caleb that you're not one of my—oh, never mind." Jane shook her head, silently praying for someone to come rescue her. This was insane, having a three-way conversation (sort of) with her old boyfriend (whom she used to be madly in love with) and her good friend (slash guy she had intense, complicated feelings about).

At that very moment, Jane spotted Alli coming down the tiki-torch-lit path, speaking into a walkie-talkie. "Sorry, Braden, but I've gotta run. I'll call you later, okay?" Jane told him. "Alli!" she cried out, rushing over to her and giving her a quick hug. "I'm soooo glad to see you!"

Alli looked totally confused. "You are?"

"I am! You need me for something now, right?"

"Uh, right. I'm supposed to take you and the other girls over to the terrace for the opening segment, and—"

"Great! I'm ready!"

"So who's Braden?" Caleb said, once again standing right behind her. "Is that that guy I read about in the magazines? Didn't you and he—"

"I've gotta run, Caleb. I'll see you later, okay?" Jane said. Then, before he could say another word, she turned to make her escape, trying not to trip on her black stiletto heels as she followed Alli down the path.

But what was she escaping, exactly? Two guys whom she used to like? Who used to like her? Who maybe *still* liked her, by the way they were acting? Or did guys always act like this, all possessive and territorial and she's-mine-I-saw-her-first?

It was a very good thing she was not dating these days.

2

BEST FRIENDS

"Yeah, so Jane and I used to be best friends. It's really sad," Madison Parker explained to the umpteenth reporter.

Madison dabbed at her eyes for good effect, being careful not to mar her five-hundred-dollar makeup job. She'd tried out a new stylist for the season premiere party tonight—some of the biggest names in Hollywood used him—and he hadn't disappointed. On the other side of the pool, which was filled with fragrant white gardenias and floating candles, a group of girls held up a sign that said, WE LOVE YOU MADYSON!!!!!!! in hot pink. *Learn to spell, morons,* she thought, annoyed.

The reporter from *Gossip* magazine—Tiffani?— nodded and scribbled in her tiny notebook. "So why do you think Jane moved out? And are we going to see that on tonight's episode?"

"Shhh, that's not till next week," Madison stage-whispered, pretending to be letting Tiffani in on the biggest secret ever, even though she had told the same thing to five other reporters earlier. "I'll tell you why Jane moved out. Everyone knows that she hooked up with her boyfriend Jesse's best friend, Braden, back in December, and that Jesse found out, right? Well, Jane got this insane idea that *I* told Jesse about it."

Tiffani looked puzzled. "But didn't Jesse find out from our magazine when the pictures—"

"All I know is, Jane blames me," Madison cut in. "It's crazy. I would never do anything like that to her. I loved her like a sister. I still do."

Tiffani nodded and scribbled some more.

This is soooo easy, Madison thought.

Things hadn't looked very good for Madison last month, when Jane got hold of some emails proving that Madison had leaked those photos to *Gossip.* Any other girl might have given up, under the circumstances. But not Madison. She not only refused to confess or apologize to Jane . . . she decided to go on the offensive, talking to every reporter who would listen about her *way*-more-interesting version of events.

Madison studied her new set of dark purple acrylic nails. The nails on her right hand spelled LOVE! with tiny rhinestones; the nails on her left spelled FAME! "And that's not all Jane did," she said to Tiffani. "Jesse forgave her for hooking up with Braden, and they got back together right after New Year's, right? But Jane was still obsessed with Braden. She was hanging out with him and having secret meet-ups, and that's why Jesse dumped her again. And now she's not speaking to me, like it's my fault she cheated on her boyfriend."

Tiffani whistled. "Wow, this is great stuff."

Madison smiled smugly. "I know." She didn't tell Tiffani that she'd left out a few important details, like the fact that Jane and Braden only had one "secret meet-up"—a very public lunch at Barney Greengrass—or that Jane told Jesse about it herself, the same night.

Tiffani glanced up from her notepad. "Anything else?"

"I think that's all. You'll be the first to know if something else comes up," Madison lied. "Soooo. When's this story going to run?"

"Veronica told me to tell you she's clearing space for this week's edition. And if there's a follow-up story, one of us may be calling you for quotes."

"Awesome."

Veronica Bliss, the editor in chief of *Gossip*, was really coming through for Madison lately. (Madison had spotted Veronica at the party earlier, having an intense-looking convo with Trevor. She had also spotted Veronica's former assistant Diego—the rat who had dug up the incriminating emails against Madison—chatting up a publicist, presumably to get dish for his annoying new blog, D-Lish.) Veronica and Madison had had a long-standing arrangement: dirt on Jane in exchange for flattering pieces about Madison in the magazine. Madison had made that deal with Veronica last fall because she wasn't enjoying anywhere near the fame she deserved. Back then, all anyone could talk about was Jane, Jane, Jane. Puke! Madison had been forced to help things along a bit by making sure the world knew what a pathetic mess their perfect, all-American princess really was.

And it was working. Trevor had already talked to Madison about giving her more airtime this season, which must mean that he planned to give Jane *less*. Madison was all over the media, too. Not only *Gossip* but the other major tabloids were clamoring to interview her—about the show and her rift with Jane, sure, but also about her opinions on fashion, her love life (she was careful not to mention her current, very married boyfriend, Derek), and more. It was a huge change from a few months ago, when she could barely get editors and reporters to return her calls.

As Tiffani wrote down some final notes, Madison fluffed her long, platinum blond hair and gazed out at her adoring fans. She *assumed* they were her fans, anyway; after all, Jane was old news, Scarlett was a complete freak, and Gaby was . . . well, she was about as interesting as last year's diet fad.

A tall girl wearing a sorry-looking boyfriend shirt over leggings came running up to her. "Oh, there you are!" she said, panting. "I've been looking all over for you. You need to get over to the terrace, like, ASAP."

"Who are you?" Madison snapped. "Can't you see I'm busy?"

"I'm Alli. From the show. We're about to go live,

and they need you and the other girls to do the opening segment."

"Oh!"

Madison said a hasty good-bye to Tiffani and followed Alli in the direction of the terrace. She wished she could check herself in a mirror, although she knew they'd have stylists waiting to touch her up. Besides, what was she worried about? She looked amazing in her shimmering purple tank dress that hugged her perfect size-0 body. She *felt* amazing, too. Tonight was the start of a brand-new season: *her* season. She was on a roll, and nothing was going to stop her.

When her cell buzzed as she hurried to the terrace, she pulled it out quickly and checked the screen. It was a text from a private number.

Madison frowned. It couldn't be from *that person* . . . could it? Biting back her anxiety, she clicked on the message.

WHY R U IGNORING MY TEXTS? I TOLD U I WOULD GIVE U 30 DAYS TO COME UP WITH THE MONEY. WELL YOUR 30 DAYS ARE UP SO NOW IM HERE TO COLLECT IN PERSON. BTW PURPLE ISNT YOUR COLOR.

Madison stopped in her tracks and gazed wildly around the crowd. Was the person here, tonight, watching her? How could that be? She scanned the sea of faces, but no one stood out. A *Hollywood Now* TV camera zoomed in on her, then swiveled away. A couple of girls took pictures of her with their cell phones, and another one yelled, "Ohmigod, will you autograph my shirt?" The girl's red tee said TEAM MADISON across the front of it.

Normally, Madison would have stopped to chat up such a devoted fan. But the text had thrown her. She'd been getting these messages for months now. At first whoever sent them hinted at knowing "who Madison really was," and then actually mailed Madison a school picture of herself from five years ago: when she was fifteen, and not so attractive, and not going by the name of Madison Parker.

"Madison? We kinda need to rush here," Alli called out to her.

"Huh? Oh, right." Madison took a Sharpie out of her silver clutch and scrawled her name quickly on the girl's shirt. "Thanks for watching the show," she said without taking her eyes off the crowd. But what was she looking for? She didn't have a single clue about her blackmailer's appearance, despite having hired a private detective to track the person down. Unfortunately, he had nothing yet.

"Ohmigod, she wrote on my shirt!" the girl screamed to her friends.

Madison tried to forget about the text as Alli led her to the terrace, where a couple of PopTV cameramen were setting up, and Dana and a director named Matt were barking orders at the sound and light guys. Half a dozen stylists were busily touching up Gaby, Scarlett, and . . . Jane. Ugh. As if Madison didn't have enough to worry about right now. Jane, who looked almost fat in her ruffly black dress (well, maybe "fat" was an exaggeration), barely glanced her way. *Whatever, bitch,* Madison thought, narrowing her eyes. Still, it was getting ridiculous, their not talking to each other. She was going to have to do something about that.

"Madison, there you are." Out of nowhere, Trevor Lord sauntered up to her, looking suave and sophisticated as always in a tailored black suit and white shirt, no tie. "Did Dana fill you in already?"

Madison shook her head. "About what?"

Trevor put a hand on her elbow. "We need you four girls to do the intro segment together, then maybe one or two more after that. We were originally going to have it be Jane and Scarlett on the terrace, then cut away to you and Gaby at the pool . . . but, well, change of plans." He lowered his voice and added, "Sorry, they sprung this on me. Is it going to be okay with the two of you up there together?"

"*I'm* not going to be the problem," Madison huffed.

"Good. I need you to behave, okay? Just read what's on the teleprompter. Remember, this is live."

"You know I always do whatever you say, Trevor." Madison smiled sweetly at him.

Trevor smiled back. "Yes, I know. In fact, I have

20

something I want to discuss with you. A new idea for this season. It'll mean a lot more work for you, though."

"More work? You mean, like my own story line?"

"Exactly."

"Trevor, I love you!" Madison had to keep herself from throwing her arms around him and jumping up and down with joy. "So what is it? Am I going to have a new boyfriend or a new job or—"

"I'll fill you in after this segment. Now go get miked. We're live in five."

Five minutes later, Madison found herself in front of the PopTV cameras, sandwiched between Jane and Gaby, with Scarlett on the other side of Jane. She blinked into the bright, hot glare of the lights and tried to focus on the task at hand—but it wasn't easy. All she could think about was what Trevor had said to her. Her own story line! It was a dream come true.

Then everything began happening at once: Matt, the director, gave the five-second countdown . . . and the crowd began to cheer . . . and Jane turned away from the cameras and the teleprompter and toward Madison. "Hey, I think we're on the air!" she recited, fake-smiling.

Madison fake-smiled back. Nauseating. "I think you're right!"

Jane faced forward again. "Welcome to the *L.A. Candy* Season Two premiere party, everybody!" she said, stage-clapping. (Cue: more crowd cheers.)

"I thought it was Season *Three*," Gaby said, squinting at the teleprompter. (Cue: crowd laughter.)

"Oh, Gaby!" Scarlett said, rolling her eyes. (Cue: more crowd laughter.)

God, who writes this stuff? Madison wondered drily. *It's soooo cheesy.*

"We have lots of surprises lined up for you tonight," Jane said.

Madison started to read her next line, then did a double-take at the teleprompter. Were they seriously asking her to say *that*? "Yeah, *lots* of surprises," she recited. "Like what's going to happen this season with me and my best friend Jane." The teleprompter then instructed her to "bump lightly into Jane," so she did. She could feel Jane's body stiffen.

"You mean me and *my* best friend Jane," Scar read, bumping into Jane from the other side.

"They sprung this on me," my ass, Madison thought irritably.

"We have Aja here with us tonight to sing her brand-new hit single, 'I Need You Now,'" Jane said, pretending to ignore both girls. Cheers, applause.

Gaby raised her hand. *"I'm* gonna sing, too!"

Madison, Jane, and Scarlett turned to Gaby. *"You're* gonna sing?" Scarlett asked, pretending to be shocked.

"Yeah, I'm gonna channel my inner Aja," Gaby said.

But she misread the teleprompter, pronouncing the word "channel" like "Chanel," the fashion designer. The crowd laughed, not on cue.

"Uh, Gaby . . . you mean *channel*?" Scarlett corrected her, improvising.

Jane fake-smiled again. "Stay tuned, because after the commercial break, we'll be back to talk about—"

"Who hooks up with who in Season Two," Madison finished, stage-winking.

"Really? Who do *I* hook up with?" Gaby said eagerly. Cheers, laughter, applause.

"And . . . cut." Matt, the director, made a motion with his hands. "Great job, girls. Stand by for the next segment, okay? We're moving over to the statue garden. You can touch up now if you'd like."

The four girls dispersed into small clusters of stylists and clouds of hair spray. Madison scanned the crowd as one of the stylists applied powder to her face. She still felt uneasy thinking that someone might be watching her and having no idea who it was.

She noticed Trevor standing nearby, talking to Dana and pointing to something on a computer monitor. Madison caught his eye, and he sauntered over to her.

"Good work," he complimented her.

Madison waved the stylist away and tucked her arm through Trevor's. "Can we talk about my big story line now?" she said in a low, eager voice.

Trevor nodded and signaled for her to click off her microphone. "Walk with me, and I'll fill you in. We're looking to start shooting these new scenes the day after tomorrow. . . ."

Madison put the blackmailer out of her mind—for now—and listened intently to Trevor's pitch.

3

SECOND CHANCES . . .
SECOND THOUGHTS

Scarlett kicked off her very uncomfortable, very expensive—
not that she had to pay for them—strappy gold sandals and
leaned back on the couch. The series premiere, which
she'd TiVo'd because she'd missed the private PopTV
screening earlier, flashed across her TV screen: the opening credits, with Jane at her event-planning job . . . then
Madison shopping . . . Scarlett walking through the USC
campus . . . Gaby at the gym . . . then all four girls dancing
at a club, goofing around, and laughing. The producers
had been forced to dig up some unused footage from early
last season, when they could all stand to be in the same
room together.

"I hate these shoes," she complained to Liam Ferguson, her boyfriend (although she was still getting used to
thinking of him that way, since she'd never really had a
boyfriend before).

"Really? You look hot in them." Liam leaned over

to kiss her neck, nearly spilling a bowl of popcorn in the process.

Scarlett blushed. Liam was just about the only person in the world who could make her blush. "Thanks. Soooo. I missed you at the party tonight."

"I'm sorry I wasn't there," Liam said sincerely. "Was it fun?"

"I guess? They rented some insane house on Mulholland Drive for it. Mostly, it was a lot of talking to fans and posing for cameras and telling reporters the same things over and over again. 'Are you and Jane going to make up?' 'You'll have to watch and see!' 'Do you think Jane and Jesse will get back together?' 'You'll have to watch and see!' 'Will you and Madison ever get along?' 'You'll have to watch and see!'" Scarlett laughed. "So you didn't miss a whole lot."

Liam laughed, too. "Apparently not."

They cuddled closer and lapsed into silence as the episode, called "Second Chances . . . Second Thoughts," began. In the opening scene, Jane and Jesse were back together, but things were clearly tense between them as he griped about having to go to yet another one of her "events." In the scene after that, at a spa, Madison and Gaby discussed Jane and Jesse's relationship, with Madison remarking that even though they were back together, Jane was still hung up on "the guy she cheated on Jesse with." Everyone who read a tabloid or had access to the internet knew that "the guy" was Braden James, although he couldn't *be named* on the show since he refused to *be* on the show. Madison also informed Gaby that Jane unfairly blamed her, Madison, for Jesse finding out about "the guy" in the first place. Huh? That made no sense whatsoever. And when did this spa convo even take place? Gaby would have told Scarlett about it—wouldn't she?

Of course, Scarlett knew there would be a disconnect between this episode and the girls' "real lives." A lot of the early Season 2 footage had been shot weeks or months ago, then edited by Trevor to create a narrative flow. The Season 1 finale, which aired in January, had ended with a teaser about whether Jane and Jesse would get back together or not. In the meantime, Jane and Jesse had already gotten back together, then broken up again. Jane hadn't confirmed their split with the press because it hadn't "happened" on Season 2 yet. Similarly, Jane had already moved out of Madison's apartment and back in with Scarlett. Jane wasn't allowed to talk about that to the press, either—not until the episode aired.

Not that any of this was a secret. Everyone in the world seemed to know what was going on in their lives already, thanks to paparazzi and tabloids.

Liam curled his hand around Scarlett's, and she rested her head on his shoulder. On the screen, Jane was having an argument with Madison about Jane's new dog, Tucker, and how he had chewed through another pair of Madison's prized Manolos.

"Fascinating stuff," Liam joked, reaching into the

popcorn bowl. Tucker got up from his favorite spot on the living room floor and stared at Liam, sniffing hopefully, totally oblivious to the drama he was creating on TV. "No offense, but I'm kind of glad I'm not working on the show anymore."

Scarlett punched him on the arm. "What? You don't miss filming our riveting problems?"

"Nah. Here you go, Tuck," Liam added, offering Tucker some popcorn. He wolfed it down.

Until recently, Liam was one of the camera guys on *L.A. Candy*. When he and Scarlett started dating, they knew it was against the PopTV rules, which stated unequivocally that the crew could not date the "talent." Madison (who else?) discovered their relationship and outed them by tipping off someone at *Gossip*—and Trevor fired Liam as a result. Liam had been looking for a new job since then.

When the episode ended—with Scarlett telling some school friends about how much she missed Jane, and Jane confiding in Madison about her issues with Jesse— Scarlett got up from the couch and walked over to the fridge. She and Liam had the place to themselves, since Jane was at some new club with their friend Diego Neri. Scarlett scanned the contents: bottled water, a couple of sodas, a carton of sesame noodles, and yogurt. She grabbed the sodas and brought one back to Liam. "Drink?"

"Thanks. So are we still on for tomorrow?"

"Tomorrow?" Scarlett frowned.

"The *Inferno* premiere. My friend got us passes."

Scarlett gasped. "Ohmigod, I'm sorry, I forgot about that. I think I have to cancel. We're filming."

Liam took a sip of his soda and set it down on the coffee table. "You're always filming these days," he complained, pulling her into his arms.

Scarlett leaned against him. "Sorry. I'm just . . . you know, trying to make an effort."

"Yeah, I know."

The truth was, Season 1 had been an abysmal experience for Scarlett. She had hated the invasion of privacy as well as the fact that Trevor had edited her personality down to a bland, boring nothing. In response, she had behaved as uncooperatively as possible: not obeying Dana's "stage directions" . . . blowing off shoots . . . and in general being the very worst of her usual badass self.

After much soul-searching, and a frank conversation with Trevor, Scarlett had decided to sign on for Season 2. She had promised him that she would tone down the attitude. In return, he had promised her that he would be more careful with his editing. Her raise had been a factor, too. The money was good—no, *great*—and Scarlett was going to use it to pay for her own tuition at USC, which would help her become more independent from her super-annoying, super-controlling parents.

Besides, she saw the whole thing as a game, an intellectual challenge. Trevor wanted her to be Hollywood Scarlett? She would be Hollywood Scarlett. If they started giving out an Emmy for "Best Actress on a Reality TV

Show," she would totally be getting it this year.

Of course, her relationship with Liam continued to be a problem as far as PopTV was concerned. He couldn't be on the show because he used to work on the show. Which meant that a huge part of Scarlett's "reality" couldn't appear on TV. It was complicated—to say the least—although in some ways, Scarlett was actually *glad* she couldn't film with Liam. Filming was work, and she didn't want to mix business with pleasure any more than she already had to.

"So how are your classes going?" Liam said, breaking into her thoughts.

Scarlett shrugged. "You know. The same. My French lit seminar's okay, though. We just started a new book called *Sentimental Education*. Have you read it?"

"Yeah. Flaubert is one of my favorite writers. Have you read *Madame Bovary*?"

As Liam described studying *Madame Bovary* at UCLA—he'd graduated from there last spring—Scarlett's mind wandered to a subject she should really be bringing up with him: her college transfer applications.

She had originally chosen to attend USC because she and Jane had dreamed of moving to L.A. together. (They'd taken the year off after high school graduation to travel and figure out what to do with their lives.) And now that she was here . . . well, her new life was great in so many ways, especially now that she was with Liam, and her friendship with Jane was stronger than ever. And she *had* committed to giving *L.A. Candy* a second chance, at least for the next few months until Season 2 wrapped.

Even so, she continued to be haunted by the feeling that she might be missing out on something. Most of her classes at USC were less than challenging, and she wished she didn't feel like she was smarter than 99 percent of the student population. Had she "settled" for a college that wasn't the right fit just to be with her best friend? And was she going to continue "settling" now that she had a boyfriend?

And so several weeks ago, she had sent applications to a dozen different colleges: Stanford, Berkeley, Columbia, NYU, Harvard, Princeton, Yale, Dartmouth, and others. Only the first two were in California, and they were many hours from L.A. by car. The rest were on the East Coast. She would know in the next few months whether she got in or not. And then she could make her decision about her sophomore year. It was good to keep her options open—right?

In the meantime, Scarlett hadn't mentioned the applications to Liam, since they'd just started dating in January and things were going so well, or even to Jane, who had been through so much lately and needed her best friend around. She hated keeping a secret from them, but it couldn't be helped. She would tell them sooner or later.

"Okay, you're not listening to a word I'm saying." Liam put his hands on her shoulders and shook her gently.

Scarlett blinked. "Huh? I'm listening! You were saying something about Flaubert."

"Not. I've moved on to something way more interesting. Your birthday."

"My birthday?"

"Yeah, your birthday. April twenty-fourth. I know it's still a month away, but keep that night free, okay? And the next day, too. Because I have major plans for you."

Scarlett raised her eyebrows. "Like what kind of plans?"

"It's a surprise. Trust me, you'll like them." Liam smiled lazily and trailed his fingers across her cheek.

Scarlett smiled and leaned forward to kiss him. He kissed her back, making her feel dizzy and tingly and deliriously happy at the same time. Liam was so sexy . . . and thoughtful . . . and smart . . . and sexy . . . and, basically, perfect in every way. It was so awesome, having a boyfriend. Why had she held out for so long?

The truth was, she'd never had a guy like Liam in her life before.

So why was she even thinking about moving three thousand miles away from him?

4

ARE YOU SERIOUS?

Jane speed-walked into the elevator and pressed 5, trying to juggle a latte, a box of Sprinkles cupcakes (it was Naomi the receptionist's birthday), and her oversize, overflowing bag. "I'm soooo late. Fiona's going to kill me," she told Scarlett over the phone, which was precariously balanced between her right ear and shoulder.

"Just tell her you were having breakfast with Robert Pattinson. She'll understand," Scarlett joked.

"Funny. See you tonight? Or do you have a hot date with your hot boyfriend?"

"Nope. Tonight it's just you, me, Tucker, and an everything pizza with extra cheese."

"Sounds perfect. Ohhhh . . . my battery's beeping at me, and I haven't even checked my messages. Gotta go—bye!"

"Janie, charge your phone!"

"I know, I know. See you tonight!"

Jane dropped the phone into her bag just as the elevator doors slid open . . . to total chaos. The lobby of Fiona Chen Events had been overrun by PopTV equipment and crew—more than for a usual shoot.

"Jane, there you are!" Matt, the director, yanked off his headset and rushed up to her. "Let's get you miked right away. We've got a busy, busy morning."

"I thought we weren't shooting until this afternoon. And why are there so many—"

"Change of plans. Didn't Dana call you?"

Oops. Maybe Dana had left one of the many messages on Jane's now-dead phone. "Um. What's on the schedule?"

"First, we're shooting a scene with you and Hannah, in your office. The second scene is you and, uh, Fiona, in Fiona's office." Matt looked away.

Jane frowned. Why did Matt suddenly seem so uncomfortable? "Is Fiona in a bad mood or something?" she asked him.

"Yeah, well, isn't she *always* in a bad mood? I've got to go see about the lighting. I'll be back for you in a sec." Matt motioned for one of the sound guys to come over and mike her.

Great, Jane thought with a sigh. *Fiona's going to chew me out for being late . . . again . . . on camera. Can't wait!*

"Good morning, Jane." Naomi peeked out from behind a massive bouquet of tulips on her desk. "I like your shoes!"

"Thanks. Oh, these are for you!" Jane gave her the box

of cupcakes. "Happy birthday!"

"It's so sweet of you to remember. Thank you!"

The sound guy, Jack, greeted Jane and handed her a mike pack. Jane set her stuff down on Naomi's desk and chatted with her about birthday plans, while slipping the pack under her gray silk blouse, wrapping the wire around her torso, and handing the pack back to Jack. She barely noticed as he flipped on the switch and clipped the pack to the back strap of her bra. After six months of being on TV, it had become routine.

Matt reappeared in the lobby and waved to Jane. "Okay, we're ready for you now."

Jane said bye to Naomi (who wished her "good luck"— why "good luck"?) and joined Matt. As they headed down the hallway, they passed one of Fiona's beautifully decorated conference rooms—and Jane spotted Trevor sitting at the end of the long glass table, talking on the phone and typing on his laptop. Several anxious-looking assistants hovered around him.

"What's Trevor doing here?" Jane whispered to Matt.

"You know. Trevor likes to be hands-on. Fiona was nice enough to set up a temporary production space for him." Matt stopped in front of the office Jane shared with Hannah. "Okay, here we are. Stay here for a sec and wait for my signal, then go on in and do your usual thing with Hannah. Good morning, what's new, blah, blah, blah."

"'Kay."

Jane waited, wondering if her makeup looked okay

(she had applied it in her car, while stopped at various red lights). Then Matt gave her the signal, and she walked through the doorway.

Hannah was at her desk, reading something on her computer monitor. When she saw Jane, she pushed back her long, honey blond hair and smiled, seemingly oblivious to the two camera guys who were shooting from opposite corners of the room. "Hi, Jane!"

"Hi, Hannah! Hey, are you feeling better?" Hannah had not only missed the season premiere party on Monday, but she hadn't been at work yesterday, either.

"Much better, thanks."

Jane set her stuff down on her desk, which was cluttered with piles of unopened mail, files, clippings—and the remains of her Pinkberry smoothie from the day before. *Ew.* Jane wasn't always the neatest person, but she needed to get this desk under control ASAP. "Soooo," she said to Hannah, tossing the smoothie and wondering distractedly where she had left her phone charger. "I'm, uh, supposed to meet with Fiona this morning. Are you sitting in on that meeting, too?"

Hannah's brown eyes widened as she glanced at the cameras. "Um . . . no." She glanced back at Jane. "Didn't you get my message?"

"Message? What message?"

"I called you, like, half an hour ago, and—"

Isaac, one of the interns, appeared in the doorway. "Jane? Fiona's ready for you now."

"Uh . . . okay." Jane stared at Hannah, wishing they could talk more. It seemed as though Hannah had wanted to tell her something off camera. If only Jane could text her, but her cell was dead, and she didn't have time to sign in to her computer and get on IM. What was up? First Matt, then Naomi, then Hannah . . . everyone was acting so weird today.

Jane followed Isaac to Fiona's office, wondering what, exactly, was in store for her. Maybe it was more than Fiona's usual "we don't tolerate lateness in this office" lectures. Maybe Jane was in serious trouble. But for what? She went through her mental checklist, making sure she hadn't forgotten to do something important, like booking the DJ for an upcoming sweet sixteen party (for Leda Phillips's daughter Clementine, who seemed to have inherited her mother's alcoholism gene—better post extra security guards around the punch bowl and at the restrooms), or pinning down a venue for Miranda Vargas's (fourth? fifth? sixth?) wedding. She hadn't.

Matt was standing outside Fiona's door, giving instructions to Jack and another sound guy. "Jane! Great. Cameras are already rolling, you can go right on in."

"Okay."

Inside Fiona's office, there were three—not two— camera guys in place. Fiona herself was sitting at her desk, leafing through a file. Her sleek black hair and makeup were flawless, as always, thanks to the multiple stylists she always demanded before a shoot. "Jane, there you are.

Please sit. How are you today?"

How are you today? Now Jane was *really* confused. Fiona Chen was pretty much the scariest, coldest boss in the history of bosses. Why was she making pleasant chitchat?

"I'm fine. Thank you." Jane sat down.

"Good! Let's get down to business, then. I have a new project I'd like to discuss with you. Aja has hired us to do her engagement party."

"Aja?" Jane's jaw dropped. So *this* was why today's shoot was such a big deal.

"Yes. Aja. She wants it to be at one of the Las Vegas hotels. As you can imagine, this is a huge new account for us. Aja is an international pop star, and her fiancé, Miguel Velasquez, is one of the most popular rookies in Major League Baseball."

Jane didn't know a lot about sports, but she did know about the super-hot Miguel Velasquez. She used to have a huge crush on him, as did every other girl on the planet—and probably a few guys, too.

"I'm putting you in charge of this project. And I want you to meet your new coworker, who'll be assisting, along with Hannah," Fiona went on.

"My new coworker?"

"Yes. In fact, she's here now. Why don't you say hello?"

Jane heard the door open behind her. She turned around—and practically fell out of her chair as the familiar blonde in a black miniskirt, button-down blouse (with a few too many buttons undone), and sky-high stilettos sauntered in.

"What the—" Jane gasped.

Madison sat down next to Jane and slowly crossed her legs. "Hi, Jane! Isn't this soooo awesome? We're going to be working together!"

"No, no, *no*! There is *no* way in hell I'm working with her!"

Jane tried not to scream *too* loudly at Trevor as she paced back and forth across Trevor's "temporary production space." So this is why he was here today. She had suspected that something was up—but not this *particular* something, which was pretty much the worst something, ever. She rubbed her temples—she had a splitting headache—and she was *this close* to bursting into tears. Although she refused to give Trevor, or anyone eavesdropping outside the closed door, the satisfaction.

Trevor leaned back in his plush leather chair, his expression inscrutable. "It's not going to be as bad as you think—" he began calmly.

"*What?* What are you *talking* about? You promised me, Trevor! You promised me I wouldn't have to film any more scenes with her. And now you're making me work with her, like, every single day? What the hell?"

"Look. I didn't hire her. Fiona did."

"Yeah, right."

"Believe what you want, Jane."

"Fine!" Jane stopped in her tracks and took a deep breath. She had no choice; Trevor was forcing her hand. "Then I quit!"

There. She had said it. It was the right thing to do—wasn't it? So why were her hands shaking, and why did she feel like throwing up?

"Quit . . . *what*? The show? Do I need to remind you that you have a contract?"

"No, not the show. I'm quitting this job."

Trevor folded his arms across his chest. "Jane. I'm sorry you're upset. But Madison applied for an opening here and Fiona hired her. We had nothing to do with that, but of course we had to film it. If she had shown up for her first day of work and we had missed it, PopTV would have freaked." He added, "I don't blame you for wanting to quit your job. But look—if you do, it's going to look bad to viewers. They'll think you're a spoiled brat who didn't get her way."

Jane started to say something not very PG to him, then clamped her mouth shut. She hated to admit it, but he was right. *She* knew the truth: Madison was a crazy, lying, manipulative bitch who would run over her own mother with a bus if it would make her rich and famous. But all those *L.A. Candy* fans out there didn't know that, and if Jane left Fiona Chen Events, they would basically think that Madison had won. That Jane had skulked away in a huff.

Jane had worked hard to get this job. Unlike Madison, who obviously only wanted the airtime, Jane actually *wanted* to be an event planner and maybe even run her own firm someday. She was not about to let Madison push her out of the way now. She would just have to suck it up and beat Madison at her own game somehow.

On the other hand . . . Madison, every day? Mornings, afternoons, and evenings and weekends, too, working events? How was Jane going to survive *that*?

She sank down in one of the conference chairs and twisted a lock of hair around and around her index finger. "I need to discuss this with R.J. and Sam," she said finally, referring to her agent and publicist.

"Of course. And if you really feel the need to quit— well, I'll respect your choice."

Jane glared at Trevor. "Respect" was about the last thing she was feeling from him at this moment.

Madison was waiting outside the conference room when Jane stormed out.

"Hey . . . Jane?" Madison plastered on a faux-concerned expression and placed her super-fake-looking fingernails on Jane's arm. Jane had to resist the urge to flinch since there was a camera guy standing not six feet away.

"What?" Jane snapped, pretending to glance at her watch.

"Look. I know this is kinda awkward. But I'm willing to make this work if you are."

Yeah, *right*. "Whatever. I'm late for a meeting," Jane lied.

"Jane, you've got to stop blaming me for what happened between you and Jesse. I know you think I told Jesse you cheated on him, but I didn't."

"What?" Now Jane was totally confused. What was Madison talking about? Of course Madison was responsible for what happened between her and Jesse—or at least for telling *Gossip* and the entire world about Jane hooking up with Braden. Jane couldn't believe Madison was pretending she hadn't done anything wrong, when they both knew perfectly well what she did.

"We need to move on," Madison said, squeezing Jane's arm. "Hey, what are you doing tomorrow tonight? You want to go out for a drink? We could go to Bar Marmont. It'll be like old times!"

"Old times? Like when I trusted you and you stabbed me in the back? Yeah, those were *great* times. Besides, I'm busy tomorrow tonight, and so are you. We have a CD launch at the Thompson Hotel at seven. You should know that, since you work here. Oh, except . . . I forgot. You're only *pretending* to work here." Jane fake-smiled at Madison. "Have a nice day shopping or getting a mani-pedi or whatever you're planning on doing."

Madison smiled back at her. Jane frowned. Why was she smiling? And then she remembered. The camera guy. Jane had just acted like a total shrew to Madison on camera. Which is probably exactly what Madison—and

Trevor—had been angling for all along.

Crap!

"Ohmigod, I hate my life," Jane moaned to Scarlett.

"Poor Janie. Here, have another slice." Scarlett slapped another wedge of pizza onto Jane's plate. Tucker put his paw on Scarlett's knee and stared longingly at her—or rather, the pizza. "There's only one solution. You've gotta quit."

"I can't quit, Scar. That's what Madison wants."

"Who cares what that psycho wants? You've got to think about you."

"I *am* thinking about me. I was there first. I can't let her push me out."

Scarlett sighed and shook her head. Tonight, she was dressed in one of her usual outfits: distressed skinnies and a wrinkled plum T-shirt. She wore only mascara, and her long, wavy black hair was uncombed. How did she manage to look so gorgeous, anyway?

"You know there's no way Madison just happened to get that job, right?" Scarlett said after a moment. "Trevor totally arranged it with Fiona."

"Yeah, I know."

"Did he admit it?"

Jane gave her friend a scathing *are you serious?* look. The truth was, Trevor was more than capable of "arranging" all sorts of situations for the sake of ratings. For example, soon after the series premiere last fall, Hannah had joined Fiona

43

Chen Events, and the show. She became one of Jane's good friends and closest confidantes, even encouraging Jane to stay with Jesse when things got bad between them. Later, Hannah admitted tearfully to Jane that Trevor had gotten her the job with Fiona as part of a deal to be "Jane's office mate" on the show—and that he had instructed her to give Jane pro-Jesse advice, to keep the two of them together, since their stormy relationship was wildly popular with viewers.

Jane had forgiven Hannah; she knew firsthand how persuasive Trevor could be. However, she had never confronted Trevor about this piece of underhandedness— mostly because she didn't want to get Hannah in trouble. But now he was up to his same old tricks, with Madison. How much more could Jane take?

"Okay. So how are we going to get you through the next, uh, however long Madison lasts at her so-called job?" Scarlett said, swigging at a bottle of Corona. "Therapy? Meds? Or should we install a punching bag in your office?"

Jane giggled. It felt good to joke around with her best friend. "Maybe all of the above. Seriously, I've got to figure out how to keep my mouth shut when Madison tries to bait me into saying stuff. Like today? She said this thing to me on camera about how I had to stop blaming her for telling Jesse that I cheated on him. And then she stood there smiling at me like some creepy doll when I shot back at her. I can't win. I freak out because I can't be fake and pretend like she's not a crazy person, and then *I* end up looking like the crazy person."

"Wait, back up. Haven't you watched the season premiere yet? The thing about you supposedly blaming her for supposedly telling Jesse that stuff? Which is crap? She said that to Gaby, too."

"She did?" Jane had missed the PopTV screening of that episode, and she hadn't gotten around to watching it on TiVo yet.

"Yeah. I think that's how she . . . or, more likely, Trevor . . . decided to play this one out. I mean, he has to come up with *some* explanation about why you moved out of her apartment, right? Because he can't air the *actual* explanation, which is that Madison sold those photos to *Gossip* and lied about it."

"Huh." Jane's phone buzzed, interrupting them. She glanced at it and saw that it was a text from Caleb. "It's just, uh, Caleb," she said out loud.

"What does he want?" Scarlett said suspiciously.

Jane gave Scarlett a look. She knew Scar liked Caleb but didn't completely trust him, not after he broke up with Jane last spring.

"Cuz I saw the way he was looking at you at the party Monday night," Scarlett went on.

"I don't know what you're—oh, he says he wants you and me to meet up with him and Naveen this weekend," Jane said, reading the text.

"Naveen?"

Scarlett and Naveen had hooked up in high school, and Jane had always suspected that Scar kind of liked him, even though she would never admit that.

"What do you think?" Jane asked her.

"I think Caleb wants to get back together with you," Scarlett said.

"No, I meant, what do you think about meeting up with them?"

Scarlett shrugged and said nothing.

Jane picked up her pizza slice and took a bite, wondering why she felt so flustered. Was Scarlett right? Did Caleb want to get back together with her? He did kind of flirt with her at the season premiere party, and he acted jealous when she was on the phone with Braden. But *she* had no interest in getting back together with *him*, even if she *was* dating these days. Which she definitely wasn't. Besides, their breakup had been really hard on her, and it had taken her forever to get over him. They were in the perfect place now, as friends.

"He's new in town and he just wants to hang out, that's all," Jane said after a moment.

Now it was Scarlett's turn to give Jane an *are you serious?* look.

5

THE OPPOSITE OF A NOBODY

Madison sipped her soy chai latte and stared out at the unfamiliar Ventura Boulevard streetscape from beneath her oversize shades. Across the way from her café table was a high-rise office building, a McDonald's, and a car wash flanked by two tired-looking palm trees. Depressing. Of course, Madison had no interest in returning to this place—or to the Valley, for that matter—in the near future. This had simply seemed to be the safest spot for her to meet the private detective today, away from paparazzi, who tended not to travel to this particular neighborhood.

"Another latte?" Her waitress, a young, not very pretty girl, had materialized by her side.

"I'm good, thanks." Madison glanced distractedly at her BlackBerry.

"Are you . . . you're on TV, aren't you? Are you an actress?"

Madison froze, wondering how to respond. She

seriously didn't want to be recognized—not today. "Yeah, I wish," she said, forcing a laugh. "People tell me that all the time. I was on *Idol* once, though. During the audition part. I got cut after one round. Maybe you recognize me from that?"

"Ohmigod, I love that show!" the girl gushed.

"Yeah, me too. Sorry, I've got to get this," Madison said, pretending to be taking a call. "Hello? Oh, hey!"

The girl left to wait on another customer, and Madison set her phone down on the table. Where *was* he, anyway? He was five minutes late, and she didn't like to be kept waiting. She also didn't like having to use lame stories to fake being a nobody.

Because she was the opposite of a nobody these days. Fans came up to her on the street begging for autographs. Her appointment book was jammed with magazine interviews and press shoots. Someone from the PopTV publicity department had contacted her just today, saying that the *Maxim* people wanted her for a possible cover. A cover!

And last but not least, Trevor had arranged for her to get her amazing new job at Fiona Chen Events. Not that Madison gave a damn about being an event planner—she totally didn't—but she was beyond excited about her big story line, working side by side with Jane on celebrity events and generating major frenemy drama. The idea of truly being one of the stars of the show—if not *the* star— made her feel almost dizzy with pleasure.

Of course, Madison had no idea how to actually *be*

an event planner. But she figured Fiona didn't care, since the old woman was just accommodating Trevor, anyway. Although it was not like there wasn't anything in it for Fiona: Madison's presence was going to mean increased visibility for the company, bringing a touch of much-needed glamour and style to the place, unlike boring, frumpy Jane and that mousy Hannah girl. Fiona's client base was about to go through the roof, thanks to Madison.

A noisy black CRV pulled up to the curb, interrupting her thoughts. The car was at least ten years old, and badly in need of a new muffler. A thirty-something guy dressed in jeans and a navy polo stepped out.

"What took you so long?" Madison snapped at him when he joined her at her table.

"Traffic. Sorry."

"What do you have for me?"

The waitress began to approach the table with an eager, helpful expression on her face, but the man waved her away and reached into his back pocket, pulling out a small manila envelope. He slid it across to Madison.

She hesitated only for a second before picking it up. She was finally going to learn the mystery blackmailer's identity. Madison had hired the detective, Chris Reynolds, last month after the blackmailer gave her thirty days to come up with a quarter million dollars in exchange for keeping her past a secret. Chris had phoned her yesterday, telling her that he had tracked the person down and that he had a picture. Well, a mug shot, anyway. This was the moment of truth—and the beginning of the end of the dark cloud that had been hanging over Madison's head. Nobody was going to take her fame or her (future) millions or her *Maxim* covers away from her—not after she had worked so hard to get them.

Madison ripped the envelope open with her thumbnail (one of the rhinestones on the letter *F*, for FAME!, came loose) and glanced at the picture inside. Shock rippled through her. "No way," she said, staring at the picture. "No *way*!"

Chris leaned forward eagerly. "So you know who she is?"

"Oh, God. I don't believe this," Madison muttered to herself. "That bitch!"

"I take that as a yes, then."

Madison's head snapped up, and she focused her furious gaze on the detective. "Where'd you get this picture? Is she in L.A.?"

"The mug shot's from a shoplifting arrest a couple weeks ago, in town, but they ended up letting her go. I won't go into the details of how I managed to trace her email account. But bottom line, I also managed to trace a credit card, and as of yesterday, she was staying at one of the tourist hotels downtown. Unfortunately, it seems she checked out this morning. I've got an in with one of the front-desk clerks there, though. He thinks she'll be in touch with him soon because she lost an earring and they're looking for it in her old room."

"Fine. Let me know as soon as you have a new address for her. I can take it from there."

"Whatever you say. Do you have her real name? She's been going under 'Mildred Mains,' but I'm assuming that's an alias."

"Mildred Mains? Are you serious?"

"Yeah. Sounds like someone's grandma, right?"

"She is."

Madison told him who the girl was. Chris raised his eyebrows in surprise and gave a low whistle.

6

HISTORY

.

"Did you understand a single word Professor Friedman was saying?" Chelsea Phibbs asked Scarlett.

Scarlett swung her backpack over her shoulder and turned to her friend, who was in her French novels lit seminar. Chelsea was smart and spoke almost as many foreign languages as Scarlett. Almost. "Yep. Today's lecture was all about the meaninglessness of human existence. Cheerful stuff."

"How did you even figure that out?"

Scarlett grinned. "Because I'm so brilliant?"

"Ha-ha."

"Plus, I've read *The Stranger* twice before. It's kind of a cool book. Weird, but cool."

"I guess. I read *The Myth of Sisyphus* in high school. I think I liked that better. It wasn't as confusing, anyway."

The two girls were walking down a tree-lined path

outside of the Taper Hall of the Humanities. It was Friday afternoon and especially warm and balmy for late March.

"I'm off to linguistics," Chelsea said, glancing at her watch. "What class do you have next?"

"I'm done for the day, but I have to go downtown for this, uh, photo shoot for, uh, *Life and Style*." Scarlett felt almost embarrassed saying this, especially to a bookworm like Chelsea who probably never read the tabloids.

"Ooh, photo shoot! You're such a celebrity! Can I have your autograph? Please, please, please?" Chelsea giggled.

"Very funny. You know I have to do this, right? It's part of my job."

"Yeah, I know. Hey, it beats serving enchiladas." Chelsea worked part-time at a Mexican restaurant near campus. "Soooo. What are you up to this weekend?"

"I'm having dinner with Liam and Jane and some friends from high school tonight. You want to come with us? It should be fun," Scarlett said—although "fun" might not be the best way to describe hanging out with her boyfriend, her best friend, her best friend's ex-boyfriend, and his best friend who Scarlett had hooked up with once several years ago, on Hendry's Beach, just after someone's going-away-to-college party. And maybe would have hooked up with again, if he hadn't gone off to college himself.

"Sounds great, but I have to work till, like, midnight. Ugh. Maybe we can do something tomorrow? I'll text you."

"'Kay. Well, have a good time at work, señorita. Adiós!"

"Yeah. Have a good time posing for cleavage shots! *Just kidding!*" Chelsea added hastily when Scarlett pretended to throw her book bag at her.

Scarlett headed in the direction of her car, which was parked in one of the student lots. As she fished through her pockets for her keys, her cell rang.

Liam's name came up on the screen. Scarlett flushed with pleasure. She hadn't talked to him all day, and she missed hearing his voice.

She stopped on the sidewalk and pressed Talk. "Hey!"

"Hey! What're you doing?"

"I just got out of class. What are *you* doing?"

"Oh, making a lot of calls." He sounded a little stressed. "Listen. I've gotta bail on dinner. My friend put me in touch with this director who might have some camera work for me. He wants to meet and talk, like, tonight."

"Ohmigod, that's fantastic!"

"You sure? I'm sorry. It's bad timing, but he's a busy guy, so I didn't want to say no."

"No, I totally understand."

"I miss you. Are you busy right now? Do you want to grab food or something? I'm near the Grove but I could meet you wherever."

Scarlett sighed. "I wish. I've got this photo shoot downtown."

"Oh, yeah, that. Okay, well, I'll call you later?"

"'Kay."

"Bye." Liam had hung up before Scarlett could add *I miss you, too.*

Scarlett stared at the phone in her hand, wishing she could just cancel the photo shoot and meet Liam instead. She wasn't exactly looking forward to dinner, either, now that Liam wouldn't be there.

Because what was it going to be like with her, Jane, Caleb, and Naveen? Given their respective histories, it would almost seem like a double date, right? *Soooo* awkward.

Except that she already had a boyfriend. Who had no idea that she and Naveen *had* a history. Maybe she should have mentioned it to him just now?

Later, she told herself. It really wasn't a big deal. For all she knew, Naveen had a girlfriend of his own and would be bringing her along.

"Janie! Scar!"

Scarlett wove her way through the crowded tables at STK, with Jane following close behind. Caleb was waving them over from a booth, looking like his usual hot self. (He knew it, too—the jerk.) Next to him, looking equally hot, was Naveen Singh, sans girlfriend or any sort of date whatsoever.

Naveen was wearing his wavy black hair shorter than Scarlett remembered. His white button-down shirt and khakis made him look older, more professional . . . not like the wild, disheveled surfer boy she remembered from high school.

There was a flurry of cheek kisses and hugs. Naveen's hand lingered for a moment on Scarlett's back when he hugged her. "Hey, it's been ages," he said. He smelled faintly of some spicy aftershave.

"Yeah, it has," Scarlett agreed. Smiling, she gently maneuvered herself out of his embrace and scooted back into the white leather booth, far away from him. Then she tugged on Jane's hand and pulled her down next to her.

"What are you doing, Scar?" Jane whispered.

"Sit!" Scarlett hissed, keeping her smile plastered on her face. Now the seating arrangement was perfect: Naveen and Caleb on one side, Scarlett and Jane on the other. No one could get in trouble that way.

Scarlett had no problem with Jane and Caleb being friends. But she was concerned about Jane getting sucked back into dating him again. Jane had fallen madly in love with Caleb when they were together in high school, only to have him dump her after his freshman year at Yale because, according to him, she "deserved better" (which was basically boy code for *I want to be free to hook up with other girls*). Scarlett spent many nights last spring consoling Jane when she couldn't stop crying about him, trying to cheer her up with funny movies and countless pints of Ben & Jerry's.

Besides, Jane was still recovering from her relationships with her completely dysfunctional ex, Jesse, and the perpetually unavailable Braden. She needed to keep her life *simple* for a little while.

"Soooo." Caleb glanced expectantly at Scarlett, then Jane. "What did you girls do today?"

"School," Scarlett said.

"Work," Jane added. "What are you guys up to? Naveen, are you in school or working or what?"

"I'm a sophomore at UCLA," Naveen said, taking a sip of his drink. "Premed."

"Wow. Dr. Singh!" Jane said, sounding impressed.

"Yeah, my boy here is planning on becoming a plastic surgeon," Caleb explained, slapping him on the back.

Scarlett stared at Naveen incredulously. "Seriously? You want to spend your life carving up people's faces?" she asked him. Her father was a plastic surgeon, and she had nothing but contempt for a profession that made money from making women (and men) believe that surgically altering their appearance would bring them happiness.

"Actually, I want to specialize in reconstructive work for burn victims, accident victims," Naveen explained. "Also babies who are born with cleft palates and other disfiguring birth defects. It's kind of amazing what you can do for them nowadays. I mean, plastics is about more than double Ds and tummy tucks."

"Oh." *Well, shut me up,* Scarlett thought.

Naveen grinned at her, then turned to Jane. "Listen, thanks for the invite to the season premiere party. I'm sorry I had to miss it. Heard it was really cool."

"No worries. Next time," Jane promised.

A commotion at a nearby table caught Scarlett's attention. She glanced up and saw half a dozen girls craning their necks to stare at her and Jane. They were whispering excitedly to one another—*That's Jane Roberts, right? And Scarlett Harp? Ohmigod!*—and pulling cell phones out of their purses.

This ignited a chain reaction in the room, and suddenly, more people were staring and whispering and snapping pictures.

"Wow, that's so weird," Caleb said, peering around. "Does this always happen to you two when you go out?"

"Not always. It happens a lot, though," Jane admitted.

"So what's it like? Being famous, I mean. Is it fun? Crazy? Stressful?" Naveen asked.

"All of the above," Scarlett replied.

Jane nodded in agreement. "It's important not to take the whole Hollywood thing too seriously, though. Like, if either of us starts playing celebrity name-drop during dinner, just slap us, okay?"

"Except now *we* get to play celebrity name-drop. Like at the gym tomorrow. 'Hey, losers, Naveen and I had dinner with Jane Roberts and Scarlett Harp last night,'" Caleb bantered.

"You wouldn't!" Jane exclaimed.

Caleb reached across the table and squeezed her hand. "I wouldn't," he said sincerely. "You know me, Janie. I'm your biggest fan, and I'll always be your biggest fan. Not because you're a star, but because you're Janie Roberts from Santa Barbara who saves stray animals and likes to eat Cheerios out of an Elmo bowl."

Jane blushed. Scarlett frowned. Did Caleb have to be so . . . *cute*?

The waitress came by and took their orders. After she left, Jane asked Caleb about his volunteer gig with Habitat Builders (he was on a leave of absence from Yale so he could "experience life"), and he told some stories about a house he was helping build for a family in need in Glendale. Naveen added some stories of his own: about his parents back in Santa Barbara, his part-time job at Mattel Children's Hospital, and his classes at UCLA. Caleb and Naveen both made jokes about sharing Naveen's pint-size apartment in Westwood.

Scarlett noticed that Jane's eyes seemed especially bright as she gazed at Caleb and laughed at something he said. This was not good. Her BFF was sort of flirting with Caleb . . . and Caleb was *definitely* flirting with her. And flirtation could lead to . . . well, more.

Although, Scarlett had to admit that Caleb did appear to have changed, at least on the surface. He had an air about him: more grown-up, more together, more focused. Hmm. Could this be a new-and-improved Caleb Hunt?

What about Naveen? He seemed pretty grown-up, too, with his aspiration to help burn victims and children and all that. And he also seemed to be flirting—not with Jane but with Scarlett. He kept teasing her in a cute, funny way about being on TV (it was obvious that he, like Caleb, was not a fame chaser) . . . and making little paper airplanes out of cocktail napkins and flinging them at her . . . and looking at her with his intense, really nice (she had to admit), dark brown eyes and then looking away. Had he not heard her mention Liam's name, like, fifty times during the course of their conversation?

"So, yeah, my boyfriend, Liam, went to UCLA, too," Scarlett said, louder than was probably necessary. She pulled apart one of Naveen's paper airplanes and smoothed it out on the table. "He majored in cinematography."

"UCLA's awesome for that," Naveen said. "Does he work in the business?"

"He's kind of between gigs right now," Scarlett replied.

"Ohmigod, you *guuuuysss!*"

Scarlett looked up and saw Gaby walking up to their table, teetering slightly on her red satin heels. On her arm was some guy—late twenties?—with no hair on top, way too much hair everywhere else, and a saber-toothed tiger tatt on his right bicep. Not attractive.

"Hey, Gaby! What are you doing here?" Scarlett stood up and gave her a big hug.

"Saul and I—" Gaby began.

"Skull," the guy corrected her.

"Skull and I had a drink at the bar, and now we're heading over to Industry," Gaby explained.

Jane gave Gaby a hug, too, and introduced Caleb and Naveen, whom she jokingly referred to as "Dr. Naveen."

Gaby eyed both boys appreciatively, then turned to Scarlett. "Don't worry. I promise I won't tell Liam about your date with Dr. Hottie," she pretended to whisper, although everyone at the table heard.

Scarlett gaped at her. *"Gaby!"*

"Seriously. Your secret's safe with me. We girls have to stick together, right? Come on, Scott!" Gaby said, tugging on Skull's arm. "I think I need another Cosmo."

"Whatever," Skull said, sounding bored.

After they took off, Scarlett dug into her salad, concentrating hard on spearing each lettuce leaf precisely with her fork, trying not to let Naveen or anyone else see how embarrassed she felt. But Naveen was completely cool about the Gaby incident, leaning across the table with an amused smile and saying, "Don't stress. It's easy to misinterpret stuff when you've had as many Cosmos as she's probably had."

"Yeah, Gaby does like her Cosmos," Jane piped up quickly.

Then Caleb brought up a funny anecdote about him and Jane and Scarlett cutting class to go to Hendry's Beach and getting caught by the principal, who was also playing hookie there. (Scarlett tried to erase the image of Hendry's Beach from her mind . . . and the image of her and Naveen making out on a blanket, near a bonfire, with a full moon overhead.) For the rest of the evening, Scarlett managed to relax and enjoy herself. And it really *was* no biggie, four old friends from high school, hanging out on a Friday night and having a meal and catching up. Besides, she planned on telling Liam every single detail about the evening as soon as she got home.

Well . . . maybe not *every* single detail.

7

NOT JUST A FRIEND

"So I got an email from Aja's assistant this morning, and Aja really likes the idea of having her engagement party at the Venetian," Jane said. "The question is, how do we use that space? We're talking five hundred guests."

Jane glanced at Hannah across the conference table, eager for her response since she was always full of great ideas, especially when it came to big celebrity events. Unfortunately, Madison—whose response Jane had *zero* interest in—opened her mouth instead, saying, "The Venetian? That place is lame. The Palms is way better."

Jane gritted her teeth and forced herself to turn to Madison. Of course Madison would say this, because the Venetian had been Jane's suggestion, and the Palms had been Madison's—*and* because they were on camera. *Trevor and Dana must be loving this,* Jane thought, knowing that one or both of them were out in the hallway, listening in on their headsets. "Thanks for your input, Madison, but Aja definitely wants the Venetian," she said firmly. "Soooo. What do you guys think?"

"I think we need to have a sit-down with Aja and persuade her to go with the Palms," Madison persisted. "I'm friends with the events person there and I'm sure he'll give us a fantastic deal."

Hannah regarded Jane, her brown eyes full of worry. Jane shared Hannah's unspoken sentiments—how were they going to keep this meeting from degrading into *The Madison Show*? Because lately, Madison seemed to have perfected the art of hogging the cameras, shamelessly baiting Jane with snide, bitchy comments, and in general focusing any and all attention on Madison Parker. She had been at Fiona Chen Events for only a week, and already she was dominating the shoots there with her provocative remarks, on-camera meltdowns, and, of course, her form-fitting, cleavage-baring outfits. Worse, Madison's reign of terror was not limited to *L.A. Candy.* Jane had no idea how many more times she could stomach seeing Madison on *The View* and other shows, rehashing her teary-eyed, Oscar-worthy rendition of "I thought she was my friend and now she's blaming me for everyone finding out that she slept with her boyfriend's best friend. *She's* the one who did something terrible, not me!" Jane knew that her publicist, Sam, was working hard on a media counterstrategy. Unfortunately, the press—and the public—couldn't seem to get enough of Madison's poison.

Madison opened her mouth to say something else—then

hesitated when her cell vibrated on the conference table. "Sorry, I've gotta take this," she mumbled, scooting out of her chair. As she rushed out of the conference room, Jane noticed her reaching down her dress, presumably to turn her microphone off. What was *that* about?

Then Jane's own cell vibrated. It was a text from Dana:

CAN U AND HANNAH PLZ DISCUSS MADISON'S IDEAS?

Great. This was Dana's code for *Can you and Hannah please say mean, nasty things about Madison while she's out of the room?* Not that Jane didn't want to. But there was no way she was going to play into Dana's (and Trevor's and Madison's) hands on this. She really *was* going to have to talk to Trevor about Madison—soon.

"I was thinking that maybe we should do a Caribbean theme," Jane said brightly to Hannah. "You know, because Aja grew up in Martinique?"

Hannah nodded enthusiastically. "I love it! Maybe we could do something with—"

There was a knock, and the door opened. A young guy walked in. Jane's eyes widened. A young, really *cute* guy. "Um, excuse me. Sorry to interrupt. Fiona asked me to bring these over," he said, setting some files on the table.

"Oh, yeah, thanks. Do you . . . I mean, are you new?" Jane asked him. She had never seen him around the office before.

The guy ran a hand through his curly auburn hair and smiled shyly. "Sorry, I should have introduced myself. I'm Oliver. I just started today, as an intern."

"Cool. I'm Hannah, and this is Jane," Hannah spoke up. "How's it going so far?"

"Great. Except I screwed up Fiona's coffee order this morning. I have to remember that she likes it half-caf, half-decaf—"

"With a touch of soy milk and a level, not heaping, teaspoon of raw honey," Hannah finished. She and Oliver laughed.

Jane laughed, too—she'd started out as Fiona's intern herself, and she'd been there, done that—except that Hannah and Oliver suddenly seemed barely aware of her existence. They were looking at each other and happily sharing what had become *their* private joke, in that electric, intimate way two strangers had when they were . . . well, *connecting.*

Hmmm, Jane thought. This might actually be a *good* thing. As far as Jane knew, Hannah needed a love life. . . . And then Jane remembered that the cameras were still rolling. Was Oliver miked? Had he signed a release agreeing to be filmed? Did he realize that his little flirtation with Hannah would air in front of millions of viewers?

Poor guy, he probably has no idea what he's in for, Jane thought.

It was almost six o'clock when Jane found herself stuck on Sunset Boulevard, fighting bumper-to-bumper rush hour traffic. Braden had texted her earlier and asked if she had time to meet him for a "good-bye drink." The good-bye part of it had almost made her heart stop (she hadn't heard from him since they spoke on the phone during the PopTV party last week, and she had no idea what was happening in his life), but then she had read further and seen that he had scored a role on a feature film. He was flying out to Banff in the Canadian Rockies for the shoot tomorrow and wouldn't be back in L.A. for a couple of months.

Now, heading over to Big Wangs, the dive where she (and Scarlett) had first met Braden last summer, Jane thought about him and the stormy path their friendship had taken since that time. That first time they met, Jane had felt that same immediate connection between her and Braden that she had sensed between Hannah and Oliver— a connection that never went away, even after she found out that he had a sort-of girlfriend, Willow, and even after Jane started dating his best friend. Still, it was no excuse for her to cheat on Jesse with him, and she would never forgive herself for that, not only because of the pain she caused Jesse but because of the insane media frenzy that erupted afterward. Jane had been publicly humiliated by the awful headlines and the pictures, and Braden even stopped speaking to her for a while.

Now, finally, she and Braden were back on track as just friends. (Or whatever they were.) He had been kind to her during her last, really awful weeks with Jesse when Jesse was drinking so much and treating her so badly. He hadn't tried to take advantage of the situation or the situation afterward, when Jane and Jesse were officially broken up. Jane had been on her own for over a month now, and Braden hadn't made a move. Not even close. They'd continued to exchange phone calls and emails and texts, but they hadn't met up.

Did that mean Willow was still in the picture? Or that Braden simply had no interest in Jane "that way"? Why did she even care? She was happy being single; it was soooo much easier than having a guy in her life.

Her thoughts were interrupted by a sudden, unpleasant jolt; someone had bumped her car from behind. "What the hell?" she exclaimed, whirling around. She saw a flash of bright light, and then another—and then she realized that a guy in the passenger seat of the car in back of hers, a black SUV, was snapping her picture. He had a professional-looking camera and lens. God, he and the driver were paparazzi!

She turned back to the wheel, prepared to step on the gas (the traffic was starting to clear), when the SUV bumped her car *again*. Feeling a surge of panic, she picked up her cell and speed-dialed Braden's number.

Braden answered on the first ring. "Hey, I was just about to leave my apartment. Are you—"

"Braden!"

"Jane, what's wrong?"

"These paparazzi are following me in their car. They keep hitting me from behind to try to make me get out of my car or something, and—"

"Where are you?"

"Sunset. I'm almost at Vine."

"Okay, here's what you do. . . ."

Braden told her to drive directly to his apartment, giving her the exact directions. "Once you get to the back of my building, go down into the parking garage," he finished. "I'll text you the security code. They can't follow you in there. And then come up the elevator to my apartment."

"Okay," Jane replied shakily.

Hanging up, Jane did as Braden had instructed her, thankful that the gridlock had eased up enough for her to proceed down Sunset. In the rearview mirror, she could see the black SUV following, trying to edge into the lane next to hers so they could photograph her through a side window. She increased her speed, then made a sharp turn onto El Centro without using her signal. The SUV managed to keep up, but barely—now there were several cars between them. Good.

Five minutes later, she reached the back of Braden's building. She entered the security code, the gate opened, and she drove in. Ten seconds after the gate closed, she heard a car screeching around the corner. She parked quickly between a couple of minivans and waited, craning her neck to see the action on the alley.

The black SUV cruised by slowly and didn't stop. There were probably several parking garages on that alley, and the two guys would have no clue which one she had driven into, or if she'd simply kept going.

Jane grinned triumphantly. *Ha!*

After making sure that her back fender wasn't damaged (it wasn't), Jane went up the elevator. She took a couple of deep breaths, trying to calm down. She was fine. Her car was fine. Now she just wanted to put the whole thing behind her so she could enjoy the evening.

Upstairs, Braden opened his door before she could even ring the bell and scooped her up in a fierce hug. "Are you okay? Did they hurt you?" he demanded.

"I'm fine," Jane reassured him. "Thanks so much for the escape route. It totally worked."

"I should probably just have told you to call nine-one-one."

"I thought about that, too—except, that's probably what those guys wanted. To get pictures of me talking to the police, all upset."

"God. Okay, well, come on in. You could probably use a drink."

Jane followed him inside and realized that she had never been to his new apartment before. The last time she had been in Braden's home was before Christmas, when he lived in Jesse's gorgeous, sprawling house on Laurel Canyon, and she would run into him in the mornings sometimes. She was often dressed in one of Jesse's big white shirts, and Braden usually only had on pajama bottoms. Which had been pretty uncomfortable.

"Nice place," she remarked. "I love your decor. It's very understated." She grinned and bumped him lightly.

Braden laughed. "Yeah. I haven't gotten around to buying much furniture." He walked into the small galley-style kitchen and opened the fridge. "Beer? Wine? Soda?"

"I'd love a glass of white wine, if you have it."

"Coming right up."

Jane sat down on the blue futon sofa that along with a cluttered brown coffee table and a tall chrome lamp were the only furnishings in the living room. Braden joined her a moment later with two glasses of wine, elbowing away a pile of dog-eared scripts, copies of *Variety*, a half-empty bag of Doritos, and Clue.

"Sorry about the mess, I wasn't expecting company," Braden apologized. "So. How've you been?"

"I want to know about you first," Jane insisted. "Tell me about your movie! I'm so happy for you!"

"Thanks. It was totally last-minute. My agent called me a few days ago and said that Addison Preston was shooting an action movie and that one of his actors had dropped out because of a conflict. I read for the part yesterday, and he offered it to me last night. Crazy, right?"

"Last night? Wow, are you even packed?"

"Yeah, sort of. I can finish later tonight. After I destroy you in a game of Monopoly."

Jane giggled and punched his arm. "You are so on!"

For the next few hours they caught up on each other's news . . . and drank more wine . . . and ordered in

Chinese . . . and played one round of Monopoly (Jane won) and one round of Clue (Braden won) . . . and then moved on to gin rummy. Jane couldn't remember the last time she and Braden were so relaxed together. There was no drama tonight, no pressure . . . just two friends enjoying a cozy evening in.

During the second round of gin rummy, Braden happened to mention—like it was no big deal—that Willow had a new boyfriend who worked with her at *Alt* magazine. Jane took in this information as she exclaimed "gin!" and fanned out her cards; she tried to act totally casual about it, but inside, she felt her heart flutter. She wished the news didn't affect her, but it did.

Before Jane knew it, it was almost eleven o'clock. She forced herself to rise to her feet, even though Braden's futon couch was so comfy that she could just curl up right then and there. "I'd better go. I have to be at work early tomorrow," she said ruefully.

"Yeah, no worries. I'm sorry I kept you up so late."

"This was so much fun. I can't believe you're going away for two whole months."

"Yeah, I know. I'll call you from there, okay? I'm pretty sure I'll have cell reception and internet. If I don't . . . well, I'll talk to you in May or whenever."

"Don't be dramatic. You're going to a movie set, not to war," Jane teased him.

"Yeah, well."

Braden gazed at her, and she saw something in his

hazel-green eyes: something wistful, warm. She tried to turn away from his gaze, pretending to rifle through her purse for her car keys . . . but she found that she couldn't. He was not just a friend to her—he had never been just a friend to her—and she knew now that she had never been just a friend to him, either. She raised her eyes slowly and met his gaze openly, honestly, letting him know in the heavy, charged silence between them how she felt about him. And then the next thing she knew, he was pulling her toward him, and she was standing on her tiptoes and raising her face to his, and they kissed. *What are you doing?* she asked herself. But she couldn't stop . . . neither of them could. They sank down onto the couch, still kissing.

8

YOU HAVE TO LIE TO PEOPLE
IF IT'S FOR THEIR OWN GOOD

Trevor leaned back in his chair and stared out the window. The view from Fiona's conference room was different from his usual view: There were no buildings, no billboards, just a little park with Japanese landscaping, complete with a koi pond. He knew Fiona was inspired by nature, or at least that's the image she chose to convey to her clients. He, on the other hand, was inspired by artifice, by the unreal, by the *fake it till you make it* vibe of L.A. He loved the feeling that anything was possible in this city, as long as you had the brains and the energy and the sheer, unapologetic gall to invent it. Or to invent yourself.

Trevor knew that *L.A. Candy* was his best invention yet. And Season 2 was already exceeding expectations. The Jane-Madison feud was a ratings bonanza, fueled by Madison's almost daily media appearances faux crying into a silk handkerchief. Scarlett was cooperating—*finally*—and was even doing some media herself.

Trevor's idea about giving Hannah her own love interest was paying off, too. Oliver was working out very well so far, although how painful could it be to pretend to like a pretty, smart, sweet girl like Hannah? Still, he had better be worth it, since Trevor had been forced to sit through several dozen audition tapes to find the right guy.

As for Gaby, well, she had a new publicist, which had annoyed Trevor at first, since publicists could be a nightmare, making all kinds of crazy demands on behalf of their clients. But this one, Annabelle, had some good ideas. Gaby *did* need to start dating up; Trevor had actually cringed when he saw the tabloid pictures of her with some guy named "Skull" at STK last weekend. Gaby needed to improve her image, maybe with new hair and makeup and sexier clothes. She needed star quality, or at least the appearance of it. And if Annabelle could make this happen, why *shouldn't* Trevor give Gaby more airtime?

And speaking of STK . . . Trevor scrolled around on his laptop until he found the pictures of Gaby and her date leaving the popular restaurant. His assistant had a Google alert on anything *L.A. Candy.* All of his girls—and anyone who was associated with his girls—were being watched. They were always on his radar, and the second they made their way onto the websites and blogs, he was notified.

So. Gaby wasn't the only *L.A. Candy* girl to dine at STK that night. There were pictures of Jane and Scarlett as well, leaving the restaurant—and five feet behind them were two young, good-looking guys.

When it came to paparazzi, there was a system. Trevor was a man of details, so he always picked up on the nonverbal clues. A picture of two people with zero feet between them and with their arms around each other probably meant it was just for show or to counteract a breakup rumor. One foot between two people meant they were together and were neither hiding it nor flaunting it. Two feet between the couple, or if the guy was walking directly behind the girl, no hand-holding or interaction, likely meant that it was a new, undefined relationship or simply a friendship. (If there was enough room between the two, the guy could be cropped out and the girl's image could be used for a fashion shot.)

The five-foot buffer between Trevor's two girls and the two young, good-looking guys (who were shadowed in the background) meant that they were together. Trevor had done some digging and found out that one of them was Jane's old boyfriend from high school and the other was his best friend and a premed student at UCLA. A rekindled romance between Jane and her ex would make a great story line for Season 2. And judging from the photo, it appeared to be a double date? A romance between Scarlett and the premed would make an equally great story line. Yes, Scarlett already had a boyfriend, but since he absolutely could not be on the show, he was nonexistent to Trevor. Scarlett didn't seem like the type to cheat, but Trevor was good at what he did. He knew it would only take a couple of stolen glances on the show (not necessarily at each other) and the right pop song in the background to fabricate a new relationship.

There was a knock on the door. It was Jane. "Hey, Trevor? Are you busy?" she asked.

"Not at all. Come on in."

Jane closed the door and sat down across the conference table from him. There were dark circles under her eyes, as though she'd been up all night. It wasn't like her to party until dawn; that was more Madison's or Gaby's style. "What's up? You look like you could use a pick-me-up. You want me to send a PA out for coffee or a Red Bull?" he offered.

"No, thanks. Listen, Trevor. I know you said it had to be this way, but . . . Madison. She's just not working out."

Of course. "What do you mean, 'she's not working out'?" he said patiently. Since Jane's meltdown in this very same conference room last Wednesday, he'd gotten multiple calls from both her agent and her publicist, screaming bloody murder about their client having to film with Madison. What was wrong with these people? Sure, it was their job to represent their client's best interests. But in this case, Jane's "best interests" were high ratings, and her daily fireworks with Madison provided that.

"I mean, she's not letting me do my job here," Jane complained. "She's supposed to be helping me with Aja's engagement party and some other parties, too. But she doesn't know anything about event planning, and all she does is criticize my ideas for stupid, random reasons. On

77

camera. Maybe that's good for the show or whatever, but it's not good for me, you know, professionally. We're already behind schedule on Aja's party because of Madison's drama."

Trevor steepled his hands under his chin and smiled sympathetically. "I hear you, Jane. But that's something you should take up with Fiona. I'm just the producer, and my only role in all of this is to make sure my crew films your life—"

"But this isn't my life!" Jane cut in.

"Actually, it is," Trevor pointed out. "Like it or not, your fight with Madison is a *big* part of your life these days. The press is all over it, and I would look like an idiot if I didn't include that story line in the show." He added, "Need I remind you that you get paid a lot of money to do this? You can't just pick and choose which parts of your life you want to have on the show. This is reality TV . . . not some feel-good sitcom where everyone always gets along."

Jane stared at him, her blue eyes wide with hurt. Okay, so maybe he'd been too tough on her.

"Look. Jane. Just stick it out a little longer. Once these episodes start airing, the public is going to see Madison's true colors. Everyone's going to know that *she's* the bad guy. Not you."

"Yeah, well, maybe. I don't know."

Trevor studied her as she turned away from him and began twisting a lock of her hair around her index finger. She had been through a lot these past few months.

78

Trevor hated to admit it, but he felt somewhat guilty about encouraging Jane to stay with Jesse, especially after things got so ugly between them. Sure, the ratings had been amazing for a while, after Jane and Jesse became America's favorite reality TV couple. But he could see the toll their breakup (and makeup and breakup) had taken on her emotionally. He hadn't known how bad it really was until after they had split up.

He also felt somewhat guilty about Jesse's downward spiral. Of course Jesse was responsible for being an addict—no one else. But it wasn't pretty to watch anyone hit rock bottom the way Jesse had. Trevor had heard through the grapevine that even Jesse's drinking buddies had pleaded for him to go to rehab. And that he had refused.

Jane glanced at her watch and rose to her feet. "I've got to go. I have a meeting with Fiona at eleven, and I need to prepare."

"Wait, Jane. Have you talked to Jesse lately?"

"Um, no? Why are you asking me that?"

"Because I've heard he's in bad shape. People have been trying to persuade him to go into rehab, but he's not listening. I was just thinking, maybe he'd listen to you?"

"You want me to get Jesse to go into rehab?" Jane said incredulously. "I know you want reality for the show, Trevor. But this isn't—"

Trevor held up his hands. "No, no. This isn't for the show. I'm just suggesting that you have a private discussion with him, see if you can persuade him to get some help."

He added, "Jane, you used to be in love with the guy. Why not just talk to him?"

"Why do *you* care about Jesse? He was always about the ratings for you."

"Fair enough. But I care about *you*," he said. "I dragged you into this whole crazy Hollywood scene the night I discovered you at Les Deux. And I know what it would do to you if Jesse ended up . . . well, if something happened to him."

Jane was quiet for a moment. "I'll . . . think about it," she said.

"Okay, good. And if you do talk to him, well . . . I have one piece of advice. Jesse's not in a good place right now, inside. And when it comes to addicts, you have to tell them whatever they want to hear. Sometimes you have to make promises even if you have no intention of keeping them."

"What are you saying?"

"What I'm saying is, sometimes, you have to lie to people if it's for their own good."

Jane's jaw dropped. Trevor wasn't sure if she was more shocked by his advice or by the fact that he really meant it. Frankly, it was probably the closest thing he would ever have to a personal philosophy.

9

ARMPIT FALLS

Madison leaned forward in the worn leather chair, her face half-hidden behind the latest issue of *Cosmopolitan* as the parade of tourists passed by. She felt like a stupid cliché from a stupid mystery thriller, hanging out in disguise in a sketchy hotel lobby. Her hair was pulled back in a tight ponytail, and her eyes were obscured by a pair of last year's Ray-Bans.

Chris the detective had called her two days ago (during an on-camera work meeting with Jane and Hannah—bad timing), saying that her blackmailer had been living in this particular hotel since Tuesday and was hanging out with a touring rock band with the extremely lame name of Dead White Boyz. According to a bellhop Chris had spoken to, she was in the habit of drinking in the hotel bar this time of day, alone.

Madison checked her watch. Three p.m. Hmm, great time of day to be boozing it up. Not that she was averse to an occasional afternoon cocktail, but still.

Luckily, Madison's new faux boss didn't seem to care about her comings and goings, which gave her the freedom to skip out of work early and engage in these tedious stake-outs. And also to squeeze in interviews at *Us* and *People* and a photo shoot to benefit a trendy animal-rights group that was whining about fur. Yesterday, unfortunately, the blackmailer had never turned up—plunging Madison into a deep funk relieved only by her boyfriend Derek's sur-prise visit later that night. (His wife had her book club, and the brat was with the nanny.)

Madison set down her magazine, adjusted her shades, and stirred restlessly. A group of Japanese conventioneers walked by, followed by a harried-looking woman with a little girl and a screaming toddler. The girl reached over and offered her baby sister a bite of her ice cream cone, obviously trying to placate her. In response, the toddler took the ice cream cone and threw it on the ground. Nice. Madison reminded herself never to have children.

The revolving doors spun around noisily, and a girl, late teens, sauntered in. She was in full black goth uni-form: mesh top, lace choker, jeans with metal rings, and platform boots. Her hair hung unevenly to her shoulders, as though hacked by a meat cleaver.

She looked crazier than she had in her mug shot.

The girl headed for the bar, just off the lobby. Madison got up and followed her, observing from a distance as she sat down on a barstool and ordered a shot of vodka from the bartender. The guy barely glanced at her, even though she was clearly not twenty-one, and reached for a bottle of Smirnoff from the shelf.

Madison, grateful that the place was so deserted at this hour, sidled up to the bar. "Hey, Soph. Didn't know you were in town. You really should have called," she said sweetly.

Sophie whirled around and stared at Madison in shock. Up close, her little sister looked even more freakish, with her bruise-colored eye shadow and plum lipstick. Still, underneath the getup, she was the same, infuriatingly beautiful Sophie from five years ago. (She had always been partial to fads, even as a kid; obviously, she was going through her goth fad now.)

Without a word, Sophie turned away from Madison and tipped back her drink, which the bartender had set down in front of her. "Another one," she told him gruffly.

"What's the matter, Soph? You've never been the quiet type before," Madison said.

"What are you doing here?"

"I'm here to find out why you've been trying to make my life miserable these last few months."

"*I've* been trying to make *your* life miserable? You're the one who left me alone in Armpit Falls, bitch."

Madison sat down next to her and waved away the bartender. "What do you mean, alone? What about Mom?"

Sophie snorted. "Yeah, that's hilarious."

"How is she?"

"She's awesome, thanks for asking. I can't wait to get home so I can go back to picking her off the floor every night and cleaning up her vomit. And lying to those bill collectors on the phone because she's too wasted to keep a fucking job."

Madison winced. She remembered their mother's drinking binges all too well. And she felt a stab of sympathy for Sophie, dealing with it all by herself. But the feeling vanished as soon as she remembered why she was here. "Yeah, so your solution was to blackmail me?" she said.

Sophie narrowed her eyes. "You left us. You disappeared, and the next thing I know you're on TV making millions. Yeah, I recognized you. Maybe nobody else did, but I did. And you never even called." She added, "You walk around in your Gucci shoes acting so much better than everyone . . . that's two months' rent, Maddy. You're walking around on two months' rent."

"I'm making millions?" Madison laughed bitterly. "You have no idea what you're talking about. Every cent I've made from filming has gone to pay off my credit card debt. The debt I built up trying to keep up this . . . *image*. I'm basically broke."

"Don't lie to me. I want my quarter million, and I want it now. Or I'm telling the entire world the truth. You're not Madison Parker—you're Madelyn Wardell."

Madison bristled. "Do . . . not . . . call . . . me . . . that."

"Why not? That's your real name."

"Not anymore."

Sophie smiled meanly. "Yeah, well, I don't think your fans are going to be too stoked when they find out you're a total fraud. I've read the magazines and I've watched you on the talk shows. You're running around pretending you're some high-society heiress who went to boarding schools in Europe or whatever. Wait'll they find out you're a nobody who grew up in a trailer park in Armor Falls, New York . . . who ran away from home when she was fifteen and got a ton of plastic surgery so nobody would know how fat and ugly she was."

"Don't talk to me like that!"

Madison clenched her fists to keep herself from slapping Sophie. How dare she. How *dare* she! Sophie had no idea what she had been through all these years. Growing up in that depressing little town with a chronically drunk mom had been bad enough. On top of which she had been cursed with a weight problem, bad skin, mousy hair, and a big nose. Unlike Sophie, who had been born practically perfect, with her slim figure, massive boobs, gorgeous cheekbones, and naturally plump lips—not to mention her pale blond hair and luminous violet-blue eyes. It was so unfair.

Madison always knew that she was meant for a better life. She may have been plain on the outside; but inside, she felt like a glamorous actress or model or pop star, just waiting to emerge from her shell. And so she had made plans, carefully squirreling away her babysitting money and her measly paychecks from Wendy's. By her fifteenth birthday, she had saved enough for a one-way bus ticket to Los Angeles, plus a little extra to live on. When she left, she didn't tell a soul.

Once in L.A., Madison lied about her age and managed to get an under-the-table job sweeping hair and making coffee at a modest salon. The owner liked her and gave Madison her first decent haircut, highlights, and spray-tanning for free.

By her sixteenth birthday, Madison was a full-fledged platinum blond; she was also thirty pounds thinner, mostly because she could barely afford groceries. At which point Sugar Daddy #1 came along—being forty-something and married, he was willing to overlook the fact that Madison wasn't a perfect California beauty (yet)—and introduced her to the world of cosmetic surgery. It was his idea, paying for those initial treatments: lip-plumping, breast enhancement, nose reduction, cheeks. Seemingly over-night (although the recovery actually took days, weeks, even months), Madison was transformed from an ugly-ish duckling into a glorious swan—the swan she always knew she was, inside. It was the way it was supposed to be.

And so began the upward climb—more (and better) sugar daddies, more (and better) procedures, more (and better) . . . *everything*. For her eighteenth birthday, she gave herself a new name: Madison Parker, after Madison Avenue and Park Avenue in New York City, where the rich and powerful people lived. It was a classy name, befitting her new image. She'd made it legal and everything.

It had taken Madison years to get from there to here, from her miserable existence in Armor Falls to her fabulous new life in Hollywood. And now her psychotic little sister was threatening to take it all away? Madison *had* to bring her around, and fast.

"Sophie, listen—" Madison began.

Sophie swiped at her mouth with the back of her hand and rose to her feet. "Forget it. I'm outta here. You've got twenty-four hours to give me the money or I'm calling your favorite magazine. *Gossip*, right? Meet me here tomorrow, same time, with the cash."

"Are you out of your mind?" Madison snapped. "I told you before. I don't have that kind of money."

"Not my problem. Later, bitch."

Madison took a deep breath. "Wait. I have another idea."

"Sorry, not interested."

"No, *listen!*" Madison knew she was probably about to make a huge mistake, suggesting this. But what choice did she have? She couldn't let Sophie go to the media. "You could be on the show with me," she blurted out. "I could talk to Trevor. He's the producer, the head guy. You could be my little sister, except we'll get you a makeover so you don't look like . . . *that*. Or like Sophilyn Wardell, either. You can have just enough work done so no one back home will recognize you."

Sophie crossed her arms over her chest. "Why would

I want to be on your stupid TV show with you?" she said.

"Because then you'll have what I have. You'll matter! And every guy on the planet will want to date you! And okay, so maybe I'm not a millionaire. Yet. But I will be, someday, if things keep going the way they're going. You could have that, too!"

Sophie seemed to consider this.

"Well?" Madison said.

"Maybe. I'll think about it."

"Great! Come on, let me buy you another drink."

"Fine."

Sophie sat back down and signaled to the bartender, who was across the room wiping down some tables. Madison dug into her purse for some cash, wondering why her hand was shaking. She told herself to take some more deep breaths and chill, already. She had come up with the perfect plan to keep Sophie from spilling her secret to the entire world. Now all she had to do was persuade Sophie to agree; then she would finally—*finally*—be safe.

So why did she have a sick, sinking feeling in the pit of her stomach?

10

SO WHO'S THE GUY?

Scarlett studied the lunch menu at the übertrendy new vegetarian restaurant with the unpronounceable name, trying not to make faces at the prices for the entrees. (Twenty-four dollars for something called Green Tea-Infused Tofu?) PopTV was filming her girls' lunch with Gaby today, and she planned to be on her very best behavior. Well, best-ish, anyway.

"Hey, Scarlett!"

Scarlett glanced up and spotted Gaby weaving her way through the tightly packed outdoor tables. She frowned in confusion. Gaby looked . . . different. Her light brown hair was longer. How had it grown six inches since STK, less than two weeks ago? It was also puffier and streaked with new ash blond highlights that screamed "look at my hair!" Her yellow minidress was trampy, unlike her usual pretty, tasteful attire. And her skin tone was several shades darker; either she'd spent some quality time in the sun recently, or she'd been hitting the self-tanning products in a major way.

And what was going on with her face? Her lips looked *fatter*, as though she'd had an allergic reaction to something. She was wearing an insane amount of makeup, too—nearly as much as Madison.

Scarlett recalled Gaby saying something recently about hiring a new publicist—Annette? Annabelle?—who wanted to "update" Gaby's image. Too bad they went for "Hollywood fembot."

"Sorry I'm late!" Gaby air-kissed Scarlett before Scarlett had a chance to stand up and give her a hug. Huh? When had they gone from hugging to air-kissing? Wasn't that like going backward, friendship-wise?

Gaby sat down and set her massive gold Chanel bag on her lap. Scarlett did a double take. There was a tiny creature inside the bag. A tiny, *ugly* creature. "Uh, Gaby? What's that?"

"What? Oh! That's Princess Baby, my Chihuahua. I can't believe you guys have never met!" Gaby scooped up the dog and thrust it at Scarlett. "Go on, Princess Baby, give your auntie Scarlett a big kiss!"

Scarlett turned away. "No, no! No doggie kisses! I don't want to give Princess Baby my cold!" she improvised. She didn't mind getting tongue-mauled by Tucker, but Princess Baby wasn't her type.

"It's time for her nap, anyway." Gaby returned Princess Baby to her purse. "Soooo. How are you?"

"Fine. You look, um . . . different. I mean, you look *great!*" Scarlett reminded herself to be nice, for the cameras. This wasn't the time or the place to interrogate Gaby about her Madison-style makeover.

Gaby beamed. "Really? Thanks! You look great, too! It's probably cuz of your new boyfriend, right? Dr. Hottie?" She winked at Scarlett.

"*Gaby!* I *don't* have a new boyfriend!" Scarlett glared at her friend and then at the cameras. "So have you been to this place before? What's good?" she said, hoping to change the subject fast.

"Oh, I don't know. I'm just gonna have a tiny, itty-bitty salad and a big, huge glass of water with a slice of lemon. I'm trying to lose ten pounds," Gaby said, shrugging.

"What? Why? You look fine the way you are."

"Because. I need to drop two dress sizes."

"You do not!"

Gaby shrugged again. The waitress came by to take their orders; Scarlett decided on a veggie burger and a side of sweet potato fries. "So. How's work?" she asked Gaby.

"Lame. How's school?"

"The usual." For a moment, Scarlett considered telling Gaby about her college transfer applications. Gaby was surprisingly good at listening and giving advice. But it would not be smart to have that convo in front of the cameras, unless Scarlett wanted the whole world to listen in. This had to stay strictly confidential until she decided what to do, and after she talked to Jane and Liam about it.

She would have to get Gaby's take on it later, when the microphones were off. "Hey, did you hear Jane's organizing Aja's engagement party? You're a big fan, right?"

Gaby started to reply, then glanced down at something in her lap. Her ugly dog? Her phone?

"Jane *and* Madison are organizing it *together*," Gaby said after a moment. "That must be super-awkward. I mean, Jane still blames Madison for Jesse finding out about her secret hook-up with *that guy*."

WTF? "Gaby? Why are you talking about this?" Scarlett whispered.

"Madison's apologized, like, a million times, but Jane won't even speak to her! And now they have to work together!" Gaby said loudly.

Scarlett frowned. This didn't sound like Gaby—this sounded like Dana and one of her famous text-messaged stage directions. Scarlett had seen Dana talking to one of the camera guys earlier, so she was definitely on the premises.

Gaby was smiling eagerly at Scarlett, waiting for her response. Scarlett smiled back, trying to mask her confusion. What was up with Gaby? Usually, she was nice, fun, chatty, and most of all, *herself*. Today, she was acting—and looking—like someone else altogether. Like a tool.

"Do you think Jane and Madison will ever bury the hatchet?" Gaby persisted.

Scarlett thought for a moment, then said, "Hey, Gaby, can I borrow your phone? I need to make a super-important call, and my battery's dead," she lied.

"What? Oh, sure." Gaby slid her phone across the table.

The waitress came by with their food and drinks, and Gaby began picking at her mini-salad. Scarlett held Gaby's phone under the table, pretending to dial a number but instead carefully extracting the battery. She held the phone up to her ear. "Hey, your battery's dead, too!"

"It is?" Gaby looked alarmed. "But it was totally fine a second ago!"

"Yeah, these things can be soooo temperamental. Guess we'll just have to manage without our phones for a while."

Gaby peered around the restaurant with a worried expression. Scarlett tried not to smirk as she took a bite of her veggie burger. Yum. Now, maybe she and Gaby could have a normal conversation.

That is, if Gaby would go back to being Gaby.

"So who's the guy?" Liam said casually.

"What are you talking about?" Scarlett put her bare feet up on the dashboard and admired her dark purple toenails. After lunch, she and Gaby had decided to go to a salon for pedicures. Fortunately, Gaby had started acting a little more normal once she and Scarlett were away from the cameras. Although Scarlett hadn't been able to get any answers out of her as to why she was behaving so strangely. She wasn't too forthcoming about her new publicist, Annabelle, either. Perhaps these things were related . . .

Liam was driving them to their favorite sunset-watching spot on Venice Beach. She had the night off from filming—finally—and was incredibly happy to be out with him. Between the show, school, and his job-hunting (he'd landed some temporary freelance gigs, but nothing permanent), it was getting harder and harder to find time to be together.

But why was he asking her about some guy?

"I had a dentist's appointment this morning," Liam explained.

"O-*kay*. Are we subject-surfing now?"

"I was reading this magazine in the waiting room. There was a picture of you and Jane leaving some restaurant with two dudes."

Uh-oh. "Um, don't you remember?" she said casually. "That was the dinner you bailed on because you were meeting some director. Those 'two dudes' are Caleb and Naveen. Janie and I went to high school with them."

"Oh . . . right."

"I told you about it. Naveen's the one who goes to UCLA. I told him you went there, too."

"Oh, yeah. Sorry, sweetie. Just forgot."

"Anyway, I haven't seen the picture, but you know those stupid photographers. They love to take something totally innocent and make it look like something totally scandalous."

"Yeah, I know. I guess this means you don't have a secret boyfriend, then."

"Nah. I can only handle one secret boyfriend at a time," Scarlett joked. She reached over and kissed his cheek, then his ear, then let her lips trail down his neck.

Liam grinned. "If you don't stop that, I'm going to crash the car."

"Mmm, whatever."

"Okay, I'm stopping the car right now."

As Liam put the car in park and pulled Scarlett into his arms, kissing her, she felt a little bad that she still hadn't told him the whole story about Naveen. But maybe she had missed her window of opportunity? Liam had just asked her about Naveen, and she had just told him there was nothing going on (which was true), and if she brought up the Hendry's Beach incident (which was ancient history) . . . well, it might sound like a bigger deal than it was. Better to leave that story where it belonged: in the past.

11

BOYS

Jane sat at the bar of Dominic's, twirling the cherry around her Dirty Shirley and staring absentmindedly at the Dodgers game on TV. Caleb was meeting her at six, and she was early. Which was good, because it gave her some time to sort out her thoughts. She felt more scattered than usual lately, with everything happening at work, on the show, and with all the boys she'd sworn to take a break from (but hadn't).

Like Caleb. What was she doing, meeting him for a drink? He had texted her this afternoon, asking if she was free tonight, and she had replied yes without thinking. She'd told herself later that it was just a drink, no biggie, and that she would go home afterward, *alone*, so she could take a long, hot bubble bath and turn in early in preparation for two work events over the weekend and a business trip to Las Vegas on Monday. She hadn't seen Caleb since dinner with him, Naveen, and Scarlett two Fridays ago, although they had talked on the phone and IM'd. Unfortunately, he had managed to get on Trevor's radar, probably because of those tabloid pictures from STK—Trevor had asked Jane about him and whether or not they were "reconnecting" these days, which translated into "can we send cameras to get some footage of you flirting (or more) with your very attractive ex-boyfriend?" Jane had no interest in dragging poor Caleb into the wonderful world of reality TV, so she would hold Trevor off for as long as possible.

As for Braden . . . she'd gotten a couple of friendly (just friendly-friendly—not romantic-friendly) emails from him since he left for his shoot in Banff. Their night together had been amazing—they'd made out and watched silly movies on cable and fallen asleep in each other's arms, and woken up at 6 a.m. so he could pack for his trip and race off to LAX. Their good-bye had been short and sweet, with no *what does this all mean?* or *where do we go from here?* analysis. As always with Braden, it was all unspoken . . . below the surface . . . and so incredibly *complicated*.

Of course, since then, Jane often found herself wondering: What *did* this all mean, and where *were* they going from here? Willow seemed to be out of the picture, finally. But there was still the show to worry about. Braden hated being part of that universe, and Jane couldn't figure out how to date someone who couldn't (or wouldn't) be on the show. Sure, Scarlett was managing somehow with Liam. But Jane knew it wasn't easy for them.

Jane liked Braden. Really, really liked him. She wasn't

sure how Braden felt about her, though. And even if he really, really liked her back, was a relationship in their cards as long as she was on *L.A. Candy*? Probably not. Of course, her current contract was up after Season 2. And after that . . . well, maybe she would be ready to take a break, especially for a guy as awesome as Braden? (Unless that awesome guy didn't feel the same way about her . . . but would she ever *know*?)

And then there was Boy #3, Jesse. Jane had taken Trevor's words to heart and actually called Jesse, leaving him a message: *Hey, Jesse, it's me. I wanted to talk to you about something kinda important. Can you call me when you get this?* But she hadn't heard back from him. Of course it had only been a couple of days, but still . . . she wondered if Trevor was wrong, after all, and that she had little or no clout with Jesse these days. Clearly, he had moved on. Or was he too perpetually wasted to check his messages?

"Jane!"

Janie glanced up and saw Caleb heading toward her, smiling and waving. She had a fleeting sensation of déjà vu: senior year, the two of them having dinner on a Friday night at their favorite pizza place in Santa Barbara. Except then, he wasn't wearing a black button-down shirt and she wasn't wearing an LBD that cost more than her entire high school wardrobe put together. Some things had definitely changed, but somehow, being around Caleb was as great as it had been in high school.

Caleb squeezed her arm and kissed her on the cheek.

His lips brushed so close to her lips that she could smell the peppermint on his breath. She pulled back instinctively and picked up her drink, trying to distract herself from the sudden racing of her heart. Why did he have this effect on her? Especially since she had just been daydreaming about Braden, *not* Caleb?

"Sorry to keep you waiting," Caleb said, sitting down. "I'll never get used to driving around L.A. I was on Wilshire going in the wrong direction for, like, ten miles before I figured it out."

"Yeah, I've done that, too. No worries. And it's pronounced *Will-sher*, not *Will-shire*."

"God, you've turned into a native. So what's the score?" He glanced at the TV set.

"Um . . . we're the blue-and-white ones, right?"

Caleb laughed. "Uh, yeah."

"I think we're winning, then."

"Awesome. I'm getting myself a beer. You good?"

"I'm good."

Back when they were dating, Caleb had spent a lot of time watching sports, and Jane had spent a lot of time watching Caleb watching sports. She wasn't a big fan—she still didn't know the difference between an RBI and an ERA—but it used to be fun cuddling on the couch and eating wings with him while he yelled at the TV screen. Even now, the only thing she knew about the Dodgers was that their star pitcher and Aja's fiancé, Miguel Velasquez, was super-cute.

Caleb finally put in his order and turned back to gaze at her. "It's really nice to see you. You look . . . incredible."

"Thanks." Jane took a sip of her drink, turning her face away so he wouldn't see her blush. "So, how are things going?"

"Great. I love L.A., and I love my job. I know it sounds cheesy, but building houses for people who can't afford them is really gratifying."

"That's so cool. And you don't miss school?"

"I kind of do. But I chose this, you know? I can go back this fall if I want, or even next spring, and my advisor says they're going to give me academic credit for my time with Habitat Builders."

"That's awesome!"

"Yeah."

The bartender set a beer down in front of Caleb. He took a long sip, then said, "Enough about me. How are you? That night at dinner, you said things were kinda stressful at work?"

"Yeah, well." Jane began playing with her hair. She didn't feel like going into the details of these two last awful weeks with Madison in the office. Every day brought some new drama, and Madison was always picking a fight with her—on camera, of course. She had tried to talk to Trevor about it, but he had been completely unhelpful. He'd even managed to make her feel ashamed, like she was an ungrateful, snotty little kid who wasn't getting her way. Maybe after Aja's party, it might be time to start looking for another event-planning job?

"I'm handling it," Jane told Caleb after a moment. "Sort of. I mean, I'm trying to take the high road, you know? Just because, um, other people are being jerks doesn't mean I have to be."

"That's not always easy," Caleb said. "Hey, you know what I do when other people are being jerks? I act really nice to them. It totally messes with their heads."

Jane laughed. "Kill them with kindness, huh? You *would* do something like that."

"Yeah? What's that supposed to mean?" Caleb leaned toward her, bumping her playfully. The contact felt warm and familiar, and Jane didn't move away. Was the vodka going to her head?

"I didn't mean it like that," Jane said. "I just meant, you always know how to handle stuff in a funny, positive way. When people are jerks to me, I get all worked up and want to start throwing things. But I don't. I just get really quiet and angry inside."

"Yeah, I remember," Caleb said, rolling his eyes.

Jane punched his arm. "What's *that* supposed to mean?"

"I'm just messing with you, Janie. Besides, I used to like it when you got angry, because then we got to make up afterward." Caleb reached for her hand. "Remember?"

Jane remembered, but was not about to stroll down that memory lane. Luckily, her cell rang, which gave her an excuse to extricate her hand from Caleb's hand— *reluctantly*, because it was kind of nice, having him flirt with her like this. Wow, the vodka *was* going to her head, and she was only on her first drink.

She glanced at her phone. DIEGO NERI CALLING. D! D was one of the first people she and Scarlett met in L.A. Jane hadn't seen much of him lately due to her crazy schedule, although he'd come to the season premiere party and they'd gone to a fun new club afterward. She missed him.

"Do you mind if I get this?" Jane asked Caleb. "It'll just be a sec."

"Yeah, of course," Caleb said, turning to watch the game on TV.

Jane swiveled around on her bar stool and hit Talk. "Hey, D!"

"Miss Jane!" D sounded hysterical. Of course, he *always* sounded somewhat hysterical. "I'm soooo glad you picked up!"

"Are you all right?"

"*I'm* fine. Your lover is not. Sorry, ex-lover. I thought you should know—he's in the hospital."

Jane's chest tightened. "What happened? Braden . . . is he . . ."

"No, not Braden, you adorable little slut! *Jesse.* He was in a car accident. He was driving drunk on the freeway. I got a tip from one of my sources, and I just confirmed it. He's at Cedars-Sinai."

"Ohmigod!"

Caleb touched Jane's shoulder and whispered, "Is everything okay?" Jane held up a finger, to indicate that

102

she'd explain in a moment.

"That boy was asking for it, ya know?" D was saying. "I know that's a bitchy thing to say at a time like this. But the way he's been partying these past few months . . ."

Jane thought about the message she'd left on Jesse's voice mail. Guess it didn't do any good for her to reach out. Or maybe she should have made that call way sooner?

"When did this happen? How bad is he? Was anyone else injured?" she asked D. She squeezed her eyes shut, praying silently that Jesse hadn't hurt other people.

"He smashed into the center divider and there wasn't much traffic, so no one else got hurt," D replied. "I guess the accident happened this morning? He was admitted but he's not in ICU, so that's good news, right?"

"I've got to go see him. You said St. Vincent's?"

"Cedars-Sinai, sweetie."

"Thanks."

Jane ended the call and turned to Caleb. "I'm so sorry, but I've gotta go. My friend was in a car accident, and—"

"I kinda figured. I'm driving you to the hospital."

"No, I'm okay, I can—"

Caleb stood up and put his hand on her elbow, at the same time tossing some bills on the bar. "No arguments. You're too upset right now to be driving anywhere."

Jane wasn't sure what to expect when she reached Jesse's private room at the hospital. She'd managed to avoid the paparazzi outside, thanks to Caleb, who had arranged for a hospital resident friend of Naveen's to sneak them through a side entrance. Caleb was now sitting in a lounge, watching the end of the Dodgers game. He'd told Jane to take all the time she needed. He was being so sweet and helpful; she was really glad he had insisted on coming along.

Jane paused outside Jesse's door and knocked lightly. A nurse opened it a moment later. "Yes?"

"I'm here to . . . I'm a friend of Jesse's, and I was wondering if I could see him?" Jane said.

"I'm sorry, I'm not supposed to let anyone in this room."

"It's fine, I know her," came Jesse's voice from inside the room, so quiet that it was barely recognizable.

The nurse nodded and moved aside to let Jane in, then left, closing the door behind her. Jane stood there for a second, trying to get her bearings in the small, depressing room.

Jesse was lying in a narrow bed, his left arm hooked up to an IV line. His face and what she could see of his body were covered with purple bruises, gauze bandages, and blots of brown iodine. His right eye was puffy and swollen, as though he'd been in a fistfight.

"Hey, Jane." He sounded so weak.

"Jesse." She went to his side. "Are you all right? How do you feel? What did the doctors say?"

"That I'm an idiot," Jesse joked wanly.

"Yeah, well, you are." Jane reached over and squeezed his hand. He winced in pain. "Oh! I'm sorry, I didn't—"

"That's okay. Everything kinda hurts right now. No broken bones, though, so that's good, right?"

"Right."

Jesse stared at her, his light brown eyes full of sadness. Jane hadn't seen him in nearly two months, since he sort-of crashed a Valentine's Day party at the Thompson Hotel that she'd organized for one of Fiona's top clients. Jane had broken up with him the week before, after he had gotten wasted and abusive one too many times.

She tried to remember what it felt like to be in love with him. She tried to remember what it felt like to be America's "It" couple, photographed at the most glamorous restaurants and clubs in Hollywood. She tried to remember what it felt like the night he gave her a beautiful silver bracelet, with a heart-shaped charm inscribed JESSE + JANE 4EVER.

But at the moment, all she could remember were the bad times, like being home alone at 3 a.m., wondering if he was passed out in a bar somewhere . . . or with another girl . . . or behind the wheel of a car. The bracelet, which had felt so special at the time, was gathering dust in a drawer she had for crap she didn't need anymore but couldn't bring herself to throw away.

"So . . . what happened?" Jane asked.

Jesse shrugged. "Same old stupid bullshit. I had too much to drink, and the next thing I know, my Rover's practically flipping over on the freeway. No one got hurt," he added quickly. "Except, uh, yours truly."

"You're lucky it wasn't way worse."

"Yeah. I know." Jesse took a deep breath. "Listen. I'm glad you're here because I've been wanting to . . . anyway, I can't even begin to apologize for everything I put you through. I know I was an asshole, and you were totally right to break up with me. The thing is . . . this accident was a major wake-up call, and I'm gonna get help. I'm going to change. And I was wondering . . . well . . ." He hesitated, and his fingers curled around hers. "Do you think I still have a chance with you?"

Jane looked away. What was she supposed to say? There was no way in a million years she would ever get back together with him. She had learned her lesson about him—about *all* guys like him—the hard way.

But what if Trevor was right? What if she needed to tell Jesse what he wanted to hear so he could be motivated to get help? What if making Jesse think he had a chance with her was the only way to get him back on track?

"Why don't we talk about it after you get sober?" she said.

Jesse beamed. "Yes! That's awesome! You just made my day."

Jane smiled back, but it was an effort. She had just done something really nice for someone she used to care about.

So why did she feel like crying?

12

SOPHISTICATED TO SUPER–SLUTTY

Madison drove down "The Strip" trying not to get distracted by the passing scenery. She had been in Las Vegas many times before, with various boyfriends, but the main drag never ceased to amaze her: the (fake) Sphinx and pyramid at the Luxor Hotel, the (fake) Eiffel Tower at the Paris, the (fake) Coney Island–style roller coaster at New York-New York, the (fake) everything. It was the most artificially glamorous place in the world, and Madison absolutely loved it. On the street, dazed-looking tourists wandered alongside high rollers in designer clothes, and stretch limos glided alongside trucks with "mobile billboards" advertising strip clubs.

Madison spotted Jane's Jetta a few cars ahead. Jane was driving, with Hannah in the passenger seat and Intern Boy in the back. The four of them on their way to the Venetian to meet with the hotel staff and Aja's reps to organize the pop singer's engagement party. Much to Madison's annoyance—as if having the party at the Venetian versus the Palms wasn't annoying enough—Jane had announced at the last minute that there was no room in her car for Madison and her "huge amount of luggage." WTF? All Madison brought were her three Louis Vuitton rolling bags, which wasn't much for an overnight business trip, considering. A girl never knew which outfits (and shoes and purses and lingerie and other accessories) she might need in Vegas, and so Madison had brought a wide assortment, everything from sophisticated to super-slutty.

Still, being alone in the car for the five-hour drive from L.A. to Las Vegas had given Madison some time to think about Project: Sophie. Sophie had been living with her for the last ten days, drinking all of Derek's liquor and trying to sneak out in the middle of the night to meet up with God knows who. Madison kept telling her that she had to stay out of sight until her transformation from Scary Goth Girl to one of L.A.'s pretty people was complete. Unfortunately, Sophie had never been the obedient type.

Sophie had never been the communicative type, either—although Madison *had* managed to get her to admit that she'd been using their grandmother's identity and credit card (Grandma Mains had Alzheimer's and was in a nursing home) and that Sophie had known what Madison was wearing at the *L.A. Candy* premiere before the preshow went live because of a cell phone picture that had been Twittered.

In the meantime, Derek was not happy about the whole situation—Madison had fed him a story about how the PopTV cameras were at the apartment practically 24/7 for a special story line, so he couldn't risk visiting her there—and was making noises about cooling off their relationship. Which wasn't good, since the apartment was his, and if they broke up—well, where would she live? There was no way she was going back to some two-room dive downtown. Between her "job" at Fiona Chen Events . . . filming . . . Sophie . . . press interviews . . . photo shoots . . . and trying to keep her married boyfriend happy, Madison was stretched to the max.

At least Sophie's makeover was going well. A talented, discreet stylist Madison knew had gotten rid of the hideous black dye job and replaced it with a sleek platinum pageboy with bangs. Another discreet contact had performed a series of lip injections—not that Sophie's lips needed plumping, but they needed to alter her appearance. Next would come waxing (the girl obviously didn't believe in basic grooming), a full set of acrylics (she had always been a nail biter), spa appointments (had she never considered a regular skin care regimen?), contact lenses (green? brown?)—and last but not least, new clothes and new makeup. A nose job would have been the perfect way to further mask Sophie's identity from the people back home, but there wasn't time; recovery could take a month or more, and Sophie was already threatening to walk if she wasn't introduced to Trevor and put on the show ASAP.

Ugh. Still, Madison *had* to make Sophie understand how crucially important it was that no one ID her as Sophilyn Wardell—or ID the two of them as the Wardell sisters (since together, they were twice as recognizable). Then everything would be lost. Hollywood was fine with fakes, but it most definitely wasn't fine with frauds.

Madison eventually reached the Venetian (okay, so it *was* kind of spectacular, like an over-the-top Italian palace with real gondolas gliding along real canals) and pulled up to the valet stand. The PopTV crew was already there, as were Jane, Hannah, and Oliver. Madison noticed Oliver wrap his arms around Hannah as they stood on the curb, giggling idiotically about something. God, had the two underlings hooked up? Madison had noticed a certain vibe between them at the office, and more than once, she had spotted them leaving on the elevator together, at the end of the day. (Not that Madison usually stayed at the office that late. Who had the time to work when there were so many other important things to do?) Madison had no idea what Oliver saw in Hannah—she'd originally pegged him as gay, because she'd asked him out for a drink on his first day at Fiona's and he'd begged off with some lame excuse. He obviously had no taste in women.

One of the PopTV sound guys gestured for Madison to roll down her window, then handed her a mike pack and a roll of tape. Eyeing her skintight, low-cut black tank shirt, he said, "I'm not sure how you're gonna manage this."

"I'll manage. Unless . . . you wanna help me?"

"Uh . . ."

The director—Matt?—called out to the sound guy just then, and he took off hastily, leaving Madison to fend for herself. Sighing, she slipped the mike pack onto the back of her skirt. It bugged the producers when the thing was visible; but she worked hard to be in shape, and she didn't like the awkward bump it created on her back when she wore it under her shirt.

After a moment, Matt signaled for her to get out. Checking her makeup in the rearview mirror, she opened the door and emerged slowly, seductively, making sure the camera got a good angle on her five-inch black stilettos, her slender, spray-tanned legs, her super-short skirt, and her impressive (even by Hollywood standards) cleavage. She had a mental image of her fans crowding around, cheering, shouting out her name. Without thinking, she smiled and gave a little wave to no one in particular before handing her car key to the valet.

"Who are you waving to?" Dana asked, appearing with the camera crew. "Are you miked? Good. I need you to go say hi to Jane and the others and walk into the lobby with them. Then stay put for a min while we move the cameras inside. If you can, suggest lunch at Postrio. We just got it cleared, and the guys need to start lighting right now if you can get them all to go. Also, you should say something to Jane about having to drive separately."

"Got it," Madison said. So Dana wanted her to pick an on-camera fight with Jane about the car thing. Personally,

Madison would much rather humiliate Jane about her ex-boyfriend's DUI, which everyone was talking about, or her truly unattractive teal dress (some people just couldn't pull off that color). But, whatever. Madison knew it was important for her to do whatever Dana told her to do, since Dana took her orders from Trevor.

Jane, Hannah, and Oliver were heading toward the front entrance. "Hey, wait up!" Madison called out, rushing to catch up to them. "Jane, why couldn't I ride with you guys? Are you mad at me for some reason?"

Jane turned to her. Madison blinked innocently.

"I told you, Madison. It was a space issue. Next time, why don't you rent a bus, and we can all ride together with all your luggage?" Jane suggested sweetly.

Bitch, Madison thought. "Sounds like a plan. Hey, so . . . when's our first meeting? Two, right?" She peered at her diamond-studded Chanel watch. "That means we have time for lunch at Postrio. After we check into our suites, that is."

"I think us girls are sharing a room," Hannah said quickly. "We were thinking of just ordering room service while we prep for our meeting."

Madison stifled a scream. Room service? Sharing a room—with Hannah and *Jane*? Was this for real?

"We can meet in Oliver's room in, like, ten minutes—we can spread out there—and go over our notes," Jane added.

"I brought my camera so we can get shots of the

different banquet spaces," Oliver piped up, patting his jacket pocket.

Madison took a deep breath, trying to steady her nerves. She gazed at her three Louis Vuitton bags, which a bellboy was loading onto a luggage cart. Grabbing a club sandwich in Intern Boy's room was not quite what she had packed for.

"We had a couple of ideas we wanted to run by you," Jane said.

Madison leaned back in the plush leather chair and checked out the other occupants in the conference room. In addition to herself, Jane (who was leading the meeting—why?), Hannah (who was studiously taking notes like a lowly secretary), and Oliver (who was doing the same, because he clearly had nothing useful to contribute), there was Aja's publicist, Wanda, Aja's personal assistant, Anna Luisa, and two guys from the Venetian's event-services department, Xavier and Hank. Two PopTV camera guys were set up in opposite corners of the room, filming.

"We know Aja wanted 'big and bold,' so we came up with a couple themes with that in mind," Jane went on. "The first one is a Caribbean theme, playing on Carnival in Martinique, which is called Vaval. The second one is—"

"*My* idea. A Venetian masked-ball theme, which would work soooo well with the setting here at the Venetian," Madison cut in. She smiled at Xavier and Hank. "We could have the party in St. Mark's Square, with Aja and Miguel making their entrance on a special gondola. What do you think?"

Jane glared at Madison, her blue eyes shooting daggers. Madison tried not to burst out laughing. *Take that, bitch.* The Venetian masked ball had been *Jane's* idea, not hers. Trevor was going to love this and would no doubt pull together an awesome episode with footage from an earlier meeting at which Jane had suggested the ball . . . followed by footage from today's meeting, with Madison taking credit.

"We'll have to run both ideas by Aja, but they seem great," Wanda the publicist spoke up. "Are they doable, logistically?" She turned to the two guys.

"Absolutely," Xavier said, pulling something up on his laptop. "Let's see . . . we're talking about a sit-down for five hundred guests, right?"

"I believe we'd need to incorporate the restaurant patios in St. Mark's Square as a private-party buyout," Hank piped up.

As the group continued discussing details, Madison studied Jane, who was doing her best to maintain her game face and act like . . . well, a professional event planner. Madison had to give her credit. Jane seemed good at her job and was somehow managing to keep her cool despite Madison's efforts to derail her. If their roles had been reversed, and Jane had stolen Madison's idea during an important on-camera meeting, Madison would have thrown a full-blown tantrum and stormed out in a fury.

Which of course would have made for killer TV.

Was it only a few months ago that she and Jane were BFFs-slash-roomies? Madison flashed back to those nights when the two of them would stay in, wearing sweats and fuzzy slippers and no makeup. They would pig out on junk food and gossip about Trevor and Dana and watch DVDs until 4 a.m. (Jane's favorite movie was *The Notebook*, and she always cried at the exact same spots.) It was . . . "real" was the word that came to Madison's mind. Just two girls hanging out at home, relaxing and having fun. Madison wondered, If things had been different, would she and Jane still be friends? Madison's personal contact list wasn't exactly overflowing these days. Gaby, who used to be handy for shopping, clubbing, or spa outings, seemed to be avoiding her lately. (Besides which she had been totally MIA during filmings this past week—Madison heard she was on vacation in Mexico?) And of course there were the usual wannabes at Fiona Chen Events who kept sucking up to Madison, clearly angling for their fifteen minutes. As for boyfriends . . . well, besides Derek (who might not be one for much longer), Madison had a stable of faux-romantic interests—mostly models or actors wanting to get into the business—to escort her to events and fawn over her in front of paparazzi. But those relationships, if they could even be called that, were only for show. If Madison ever found herself in a burning building, she doubted any of those guys could be bothered to pull her out, unless there was media present.

Bottom line, the closest person to her these days was Sophie, her little sister and blackmailer. Which was beyond pathetic. Madison wondered what she could do to remedy that situation. And if she even cared enough to bother.

Maybe someone as powerful, ambitious, and beautiful as Madison was meant to be alone? Madison glanced at Jane, who was jabbering on about the guest list now. Madison had always wanted—and *deserved*—to replace Jane as the star of *L.A. Candy*. She was so close now; all she had to do was keep her eye on the prize and not get distracted by sentimental feelings about Jane or anyone else. And, of course, make sure Sophie kept her big mouth shut.

To hell with other people. It may be lonely at the top, but it was totally worth it.

13

BOY TROUBLE

"How was Vegas?" Scarlett asked Jane. "And I want the real dirt now, before the crew gets here. You know Dana's gonna make us repeat this conversation for the cameras, so you can give me the *L.A. Candy*–coated version then."

Jane grinned as she reached for an avocado from a painted Mexican bowl, then looked frustrated as she squeezed it. It was rock hard, which was not conducive to guacamole making. Scarlett wondered if they should just order in. So far, their dinner preparations weren't going too well. Aside from the unripe avocados, there were onion pieces splattered everywhere, thanks to a food processor malfunction (well, actually, due to Scarlett forgetting to put the top on before pressing the Chop button). And Jane had spilled a jar of salsa on the floor, which Tucker was now lapping up. It had been a while since the girls had cooked dinner . . . much less cooked dinner for guests . . . much less cooked dinner for the cameras, which were due any minute.

The guests being Caleb and Naveen. And no Liam.

"Do you want the good news first, or the bad news?" Jane said, reaching for another avocado. "Hmmm, are these things fruits or vegetables?"

"Um . . . I'm not sure. Why don't you tell me the good news first?"

"The good news is, they all loved my masked ball idea—and so did Aja, when her publicist and assistant told her about it! Yay! The bad news is . . . Madison."

"God. What did that psychopath do now?"

"Well, first, she took credit for my idea in front of everyone. Second, she told the two guys from the Venetian that she was in charge of the party and that they should contact her for anything and everything. Third, she was a total nightmare while Hannah and I were sharing the room with her, and—"

"Wait, what? You guys had to share a room?" Scarlett interrupted.

Jane shrugged and sighed. "I'm sure Trevor and Dana set that up. It was easier to film, and you know . . . more drama. The Venetian would have comped each of us a private room."

"I would have smothered Madison with a pillow while she was sleeping."

"Believe me, I was tempted. Anyway, you'll get to see all this lovely footage in a few weeks when the episode airs." Jane's face lit up. "Ohmigod, I forgot to tell you the best part! Guess who didn't sleep in our room?"

"Um, who?"

"Hannah!"

Scarlett wasn't sure where Jane was going with this. "Because she was sleeping . . . where?"

"In Oliver's room," Jane said giddily.

"Who's Oliver?"

"I told you about him, Scar! He's the new intern. He goes to UCLA part-time. He and Hannah have been flirting nonstop since he started working at the office. I guess they finally took it to the next level." '

"Wow. Good for her." Scarlett mostly knew Hannah from her scenes on the show, which consisted of her being Jane's office confidante. She seemed nice—and kind of smart, too, except for the multiple times she advised Jane to stay with Jesse no matter what. Yeah, that turned out well.

Scarlett wiped her sour cream–covered hands on her black T-shirt and gazed at Jane thoughtfully. "Speaking of guys . . . are you okay with tonight?"

Inviting Caleb and Naveen over for dinner had been Trevor's bright idea. He'd told Scarlett and Jane that viewers would love hearing stories about their old days at high school, and that there had to be some boys in their story lines—even if the boys were "just friends"—since Jane wasn't seeing anyone and Scarlett's BF couldn't be filmed. Which actually made sense, in a Trevor sort of way. Didn't it? Fortunately, Caleb and Naveen had been completely fine about being filmed tonight. Scarlett knew they weren't dying to be on TV or anything, but they were happy to help out the girls.

Jane frowned at Scarlett's shirt and handed her a dish towel. "I guess? Why? Are you sorry Trevor talked us into it? Scar, you need to change. That's gross."

"Yeah, I know." Scarlett frowned at the sour cream smears on her shirt. "Are you going to be okay with, you know, Caleb? He was all over you at STK. Seriously, I think he might want to get back together."

"No, he doesn't," Jane said, looking away.

Uh-oh. Why was Jane avoiding eye contact? "Plus, you went out on that date last week. Dominic's, right?" Scarlett persisted.

The doorbell rang. "That's the crew! Oh, crap!" Jane cried out as she stepped in the puddle of salsa. Tucker began licking her bare foot. "Tucker, stop that!"

"You want me to get you a paper towel?"

"I can do it. You need to change, right now! And it wasn't a date! Don't bring that up on camera. Seriously, Scar!" Jane grabbed a roll of paper towels and headed for the front door.

"Okay, okay!"

As Scarlett walked to her room, yanking off her T-shirt, she thought about Trevor's comment that Jane wasn't seeing anyone these days. It might appear that way, but the truth was, Jane had more than her share of off-camera boy-drama in her life. Jane had confided in Scarlett about hooking up (again) with Mr. Unavailable, aka Braden James. (Who conveniently had to leave for Canada the next day, for a couple of months. Way to avoid the aftermath or any responsibility at all, Braden!)

Jane had also fessed up about Jesse's DUI and the crazy lie she told him afterward, about possibly dating him again, to get him sober. Jane knew how much Scarlett detested Jesse, and she probably wouldn't have mentioned that little tidbit if not for the tabloid pictures that popped up on various websites over the weekend, of Jane fighting back tears as she left Cedars-Sinai on Caleb's arm.

And of course, there was Caleb. Scarlett was sure he wanted to be more than "just friends" with Jane. And from the way Jane was acting, she seemed to be toying with the idea, too. But hadn't she been there, done that already, and gotten burned?

As Scarlett scrounged through her dresser for another black T-shirt, she heard the crew bustling into the apartment and starting to set up in the living room, then Jane shouting: "Scar! They're heeeere!"

"Just a sec!" Scarlett shouted back.

Pulling a shirt over her head, Scarlett realized that she would have to play serious Musical Chairs tonight to keep Jane and Caleb far away from each other. Jane was her best friend, and it was her job to protect her from Boy Trouble.

Except . . . there was also Naveen to worry about.

The problem was, she hadn't told Liam about tonight.

She'd simply told him that she and Jane were filming at their apartment. Of course she would have to clue him in, eventually, before the episode aired. But there had been something about his little jealous moment last week, when he saw the tabloid pictures of her leaving STK with Naveen, that rubbed her the wrong way. She wasn't used to being reined in. Okay, so maybe he hadn't been trying to rein her in, exactly. But it had felt that way to her . . . like he didn't trust her or something.

Scarlett wondered how Liam was going to react when she told him about tonight. Or, for that matter, when she told him the news about *Maxim*. She'd gotten the call from the PopTV press department this afternoon, telling her that *Maxim* wanted to book her for a cover. She had started to say no but changed her mind after giving it some thought. After all, she was the new, cooperative Scarlett Harp. And magazine covers were good for the show. It was all a part of the job of being famous. (She tried not to mentally choke on that word, "famous.") Besides, it wasn't as though she had anything to hide.

Oops. Wrong choice of words. Scarlett had become excellent at hiding things.

"This looks good," Caleb said politely.

Scarlett and Jane exchanged a glance as Caleb dug his fork into the guacamole. Or rather, the rock-hard avocado chunks mixed with lemon juice, chopped onion, cilantro, and Tabasco sauce.

"Um . . . thanks?" Jane said sheepishly, waiting for him to take a bite.

"We also made fish tacos. Do you guys like fish tacos?" Scarlett asked quickly. The tacos had turned out well, and seemed semi-edible, unlike the guacamole.

"Fish tacos are my favorite," Naveen said.

"Yeah, mine, too. Janie, you remembered!" Caleb said, looking pleased.

Scarlett noticed Jane opening her mouth to say, "I didn't," then clamping it shut. The fish tacos had been Scarlett's idea, because she had a super-easy recipe that consisted of four ingredients (tortillas, frozen fish sticks, shredded cabbage, and bottled sauce) and a microwave.

Jane glanced down at her lap, then up at Caleb with a fake smile. "Yeah, well, do you remember my favorite food from high school?" she asked him.

Scarlett rolled her eyes. Dana must be texting Jane directions. She could tell the difference between her friend's real tone of voice and her *Dana is making me say stuff* tone of voice.

Caleb looked thoughtful. "Hmmm. Definitely your mom's homemade clam chowder."

"Wrong! It was pizza from Paesano's," Scarlett corrected him.

Jane laughed. "You're both wrong. I was obsessed with mac and cheese. Remember, I used to make it all the time?"

Caleb and Naveen laughed, too. Scarlett was surprised

that they seemed so comfortable with two PopTV cameras practically on top of them, filming everything. Maybe it was the pomegranate margaritas (which were kind of strong) . . . or maybe they were just naturals at this . . . or maybe Dana was texting them lines, too. Whatever the case, the evening was going smoothly so far, and Caleb and Naveen were being really charming. Scarlett found herself almost relaxing and having fun. Almost.

"So, Scarlett. How's school going?" Naveen said, touching her arm lightly.

She pulled away quickly and said, "It's fine." *You're on camera. Say something! Act friendly and casual!* she reminded herself. "I had my photography class today."

"Digital or film?"

"Digital. The professor doesn't believe in Photoshopping, so we have to learn to take really, really good images."

"Wow, no Photoshopping? That's so not-Hollywood."

"Yeah, right? It's kind of refreshing." Scarlett took a bite of the guacamole. Hmm, not good.

Naveen grinned. "Could you imagine if Photoshop was never invented? And you got to see pictures of celebrities as they really are, with wrinkles and muffin tops and massive zits and cankles—"

Scarlett cracked up, covering her mouth with her hands. "Stop! You can't make me laugh when I'm eating!" she mumbled.

Naveen leaned over as if to tickle her. "Really? Why not?" he said innocently.

"Stop it!"

"Caleb and I are going to make another pitcher of margaritas," Jane announced, standing up. Caleb stood up, too. Was Scarlett imagining things, or was Jane a bit wobbly on her feet? Maybe more margaritas weren't such a good idea. "Stay out of trouble, you two!" she added, wagging her finger playfully at Scarlett and Naveen.

Oh, God. Did she seriously just say that on camera? "We're just going to finish off this yummy guacamole!" Scarlett said as Jane and Caleb headed into the kitchen, hoping to divert attention from Jane's remark. Although that was probably wishful thinking, since Trevor would no doubt edit out Scarlett's guacamole comment and replace it with—oh, maybe a shot of Naveen's hand lingering on Scarlett's arm. Or a shot of Naveen pretending to tickle Scarlett. Or a shot of Scarlett giving Jane some sort of intense, loaded, *just between us girls* look, lifted from some random portion of the evening.

Scarlett sighed, dreading the conversation she would have to have with Liam when this episode aired. It wasn't a double date. No, he wasn't trying to cop a feel. Jane was drunk, she didn't mean that. *No, I* wasn't *drunk, I was totally* sober *and I was* not *flirting with him.*

Scarlett glanced sideways at Naveen. He was staring at her, and it made her uncomfortable.

"So I have this assignment I have to do for photography," Scarlett blurted out. "I have to take a portrait in the style of one of my favorite photographers."

"That's cool. Which photographer did you pick?" Naveen asked her.

"I was thinking of Richard Avedon or maybe Irving Penn."

"Good choices. Do you have a model yet?"

"No, but I'd better line one up soon. The assignment's due, like, next week."

"Well, if you're desperate, I'm happy to volunteer. I'm cool having you shoot me," Naveen said, grinning. "And since I'm so naturally good-looking, I never require Photoshop."

Scarlett rolled her eyes at him. She knew he was joking, but as far as she could tell, he was physically practically perfect—no Photoshop or other enhancements required. Of course, she meant this in a purely objective, artistic way. Unlike that night at Hendry's Beach, when he'd peeled off his T-shirt, and she'd almost stopped breathing at the sight of his sculpted abs and . . .

Stop it! she told herself. She stood up abruptly. "Uh, I'm just going to check on Jane in the kitchen."

"Do you want me to come with you?"

"No, I'm good! I'm great! Just stay here and eat more fish tacos!" Scarlett insisted.

The camera swiveled to follow her as she headed toward the kitchen. Camera, singular. Scarlett noticed that the other camera guy was planted in the kitchen doorway, filming. She had to get away from Naveen. She didn't want to give Trevor any more opportunities to edit her in a compromising light, making it appear as though she and Naveen were milliseconds away from hooking up. Despite his slight jealousy, Liam was the most awesome boyfriend she'd ever had—actually, the only real boyfriend she'd ever had, period.

"'Scuse me," Scarlett muttered, inching past the camera guy. "Hey, Janie, do you need some help with—"

She stopped dead in her tracks.

Jane and Caleb were leaning against the sink, kissing.

Uh-oh, Scarlett thought.

14

DÉJÀ VU

Jane sat down on the edge of the pool and gazed at the moon's reflection on the dark, glassy surface. Caleb sat down next to her and curled his arm around her shoulders. It was after midnight . . . the PopTV crew was gone . . . and the entire apartment complex seemed to be asleep. Naveen had gone home long ago, and Scarlett had gone to bed.

Or maybe Scarlett was standing out on their terrace with a pair of binoculars, spying on Jane and Caleb? Jane didn't really believe Scar would do that, but sometimes her best friend could be more overprotective than Jane's own mom and dad.

"Hey," Caleb said, interrupting her thoughts, "you wanna take a dip?"

"Um, no, thanks. You go ahead, though."

"What? Where's the old Janie Roberts who used to

dive headfirst into the surf when it was freezing out?" Caleb teased her.

Jane laughed. "She grew up? The new Janie Roberts likes to stay warm. Besides, most of the time you used to push me in, jerk!"

Caleb laughed, too. "Oh, yeah."

"Soooo. Did you have fun tonight? Was it okay? With the cameras, I mean."

"It was kind of weird at first. But after a while I figured out that I should just ignore them and be myself."

Like in the kitchen? Jane wanted to ask him. She slipped off her sandals and dipped her toes into the water. *Brrr, chilly.* Still, she made herself keep her toes there, figuring they would eventually get used to the temperature.

When she and Caleb had headed into the kitchen to make more drinks, she had barely had a chance to pick up the bottle of margarita mix when Caleb pulled her close and started kissing her. It had been so nice, so familiar, as though they'd taken up right where they'd left off. Or even further back in time, when he'd kissed her for the first time in the front seat of his parents' Subaru, with "Déjà Vu" by Beyoncé and Jay-Z playing on the radio, and she'd thought, *I'm in love.*

She'd had a crush on Caleb Hunt for what seemed like forever, dragged Scarlett along to watch him at his swim meets, and secretly hated his girlfriend at the time, a cute, vapid cheerleader named Kailey. After that spontaneous,

129

unexpected kiss—he'd given her a ride home from a student government meeting—he broke up with Kailey (who began hating Jane back, not so secretly), and he and Jane became an item. They were practically inseparable. They lost their virginity to each other (or that's what he told her, anyway). When he decided to go to Yale, all the way across the country, and she decided to take the year off to explore her options and travel, she had sincerely thought they could make a long-distance relationship work. After all, she loved him, and he loved her, and they were meant to be together . . . and maybe even get married someday.

Which is why it had been so devastating when Caleb told her last May that he wanted to call it quits. Had she been naive, thinking they could survive being three thousand miles apart? Now, he was back in her life . . . and maybe even wanted to get back together. Was she ready for this? Was this what she wanted, too? Or was she being naive—again? And what about her decision to stay single for the near future?

Jane peeked at Caleb's silver diving watch, the same one he'd had since high school. God, it was almost 1 a.m. She had to be up in six hours. "I'd better head upstairs. It's late, and we're filming at the office tomorrow," she told Caleb.

"Wow, seems like the cameras are with you all the time," Caleb said.

"It feels like that sometimes. We've been so busy at work lately. There's Aja's engagement party I told you about, plus

I'm organizing some smaller parties, too. Oh, and Trevor asked me to plan a birthday party for Scar next weekend. It's a surprise, so you can't say anything! Promise me!"

"My lips are sealed," Caleb assured her.

"You and Naveen should be getting your invites in a couple days. Someone at PopTV's handling them." Jane added, "It's gonna be huge, like fifty or sixty people. Trevor's devoting a whole episode to it. Scar has no idea!"

"Wow."

"Yeah. She's not a big birthday person—remember? Trevor thought it would be fun to do this for her."

Actually, Jane had had her reservations when Trevor first approached her with the idea last week, mostly because she was worried that Liam would feel out of place at a PopTV event, even if it *was* a party for his girlfriend. But Trevor had assured Jane that he or one of his staff would speak to Liam personally and clear everything with him. Jane really hoped Liam would come to the party for Scar's sake, even though he couldn't film, and even though he might not love hanging out with his ex-coworkers. Although . . . she wondered how things were going between him and Scar lately. Earlier, Jane had asked Scar if he was okay about Caleb and Naveen coming over for dinner, and she had mumbled something about how Liam would just have to deal because she was a "free woman." Huh?

Caleb got to his feet, then grabbed Jane's hand and helped her up. From somewhere in the distance, Jane could hear the faint strains of "I'm Yours" by Jason Mraz. She and Caleb had slow danced to it at prom. She flashed back to that night, to how long she'd spent getting ready (she smiled to herself, thinking of her long blue chiffon dress from Macy's and her rhinestone earrings from Claire's— and the fact that her mother, not some fancy L.A. stylists, had helped her with her hair and makeup). How gorgeous Caleb had looked in his black tux (she could picture him standing in the doorway as he handed her a wrist corsage of white and lavender roses, and her dad in the background, snapping away with his finicky digital camera that he kept meaning to replace). And later, during that song, dancing with Caleb and knowing that they were graduating soon and that everything was going to change. But here they were, almost two years later. Everything *had* changed . . . and yet, in this moment, it felt like everything was still the same.

Caleb caressed her bare arm, giving her goose bumps. "So. Are you free for dinner tomorrow night?"

Jane gazed up at him. "Umm . . . well . . ." She'd had lots of good reasons to decide to take a break from dating. *Lots.* But at this moment, with Caleb, she was having a hard time remembering any of them.

"You like Italian, right? I found this great place just off *Will-sher.* Did I say that right?"

"You said it perfectly," Jane said. God, he was adorable. And why did he have to have those amazing dimples?

Okay, maybe *one* date. "Caleb. Listen. If we're going

to . . . um, hang out, I need you to understand something. This show is my job. Well, my *other* job, anyway. When I'm out, there's usually a crew with me. Are you okay with that?"

"By 'hang out,' do you mean this?" Caleb cupped her face with his hands and kissed her. Jane hesitated at first, then kissed him back.

When they stopped for air, he pulled her in even closer, holding tightly. "I know exactly what you need right now," he whispered in her ear.

"You . . . do?" Jane said breathlessly.

"I do."

Then, before Jane knew what was happening, he swept her off her feet and turned toward the pool. *"Caleb!"* she screamed. *"Don't you DARE!"*

But it was too late, and Jane felt herself hitting the cool water with a loud splash. When she resurfaced seconds later, Caleb was right beside her, laughing hysterically.

"You're still a jerk!" Jane scolded him, swatting a wet strand of hair out of her eyes.

"Yeah, but you're still crazy about me," Caleb teased her.

Jane glared at him. And broke into a smile. And wrapped her arms around his neck. This was definitely like old times. *Better* than old times.

Maybe she didn't need to swear off *all* boys. Didn't she deserve to have some fun, after everything?

15

THE TWO SISTERS

"I need you to get on the phone ASAP and leak some details about Jane and Caleb's dinner date," Trevor told Melissa. The PopTV publicist was standing in the doorway of his office, stifling a yawn as she scribbled in a spiral-bound Mead notebook. "We're fast-tracking that episode and airing it a week from—I'm sorry, am I boring you?"

Melissa snapped to attention. "No, no. I'm writing all this down."

Trevor sighed. His employees were going to have to get used to coming in early on Sunday mornings if they wanted to rise to the top at PopTV. *L.A. Candy* Season 2 was already surpassing Season 1 in ratings, which meant working around the clock if necessary to keep it that way.

"I want the story to make this week's issues so that people watch that episode next week. Mention that Jane and Caleb went to La Dolce Vita last Thursday. They were 'holding hands and looking very cozy,' etc., etc.," Trevor said. "Paint a picture—you know, first love, high school romance, he went away to college, can they rekindle the flames?" He added, "Get something in there about Jesse, too. Don't talk about his DUI. I'm thinking along the lines of, 'Can Caleb help Jane get over her broken heart?' If they bring up the DUI, just say that Jane is happy that Jesse is getting the help he needs." Jesse had checked into a rehab clinic in Palm Springs and was apparently going to be there for a while. Which was good news. It occurred to Trevor that Jesse might not take the news of Jane and Caleb's rekindled relationship too well. He only hoped it wouldn't derail Jesse's new sobriety.

Melissa nodded. "Got it. Anything else?"

"Yeah, but I'm still working on it. Check back with me in half an hour. No, give me an hour. Madison's coming in at nine thirty to talk to me about something."

"Okay, then, I'm off to be another 'anonymous source.'"

Trevor used to be annoyed by leaks to the press about upcoming *L.A. Candy* story lines. But after a while, he realized that they were actually good for the show and for ratings. Viewers read the stories in the tabloids, then tuned in, curious to see what would happen: Was Jane getting back together with her old high school boyfriend? Would Jane's best friend and Caleb's best friend hook up? Who was spotted kissing, and where?

This was especially important right now, since the footage from Jane and Caleb's official first date as a newly reunited couple needed some . . . *editing*. Their chemistry wasn't exactly obvious. Hopefully that would change. In the meantime, their story line would have to get by on media hype, clever editing, the right music (A Fine Frenzy?), and Caleb's classic good looks.

Trevor knew that Annabelle Weiss, Gaby's publicist, had also been feeding stories to the press—about Gaby and Madison allegedly feuding with Jane and Scarlett—which had not only helped ratings but increased Gaby's visibility as well. Speaking of Gaby, he wondered when she was due back from her "vacation." He would have to check with Annabelle so he could arrange the shooting schedule.

Trevor turned back to his desk and pulled out his notebook, a brown crocodile-skin Smythson, definitely a step up from a spiral Mead. His wife had given it to him for his birthday so he could start "keeping a daily journal" and "learn to be more in touch with his feelings" or whatever. Of course, he had no interest in writing down his moods . . . but the notebook *was* useful for jotting down ideas about the show.

Trevor opened it to a clean page and wrote:

S & N. (Same episode as La Dolce Vita date.)

Underneath, he wrote:

(1) C & N came over to J & S's apt. last Wednesday for an intimate dinner party. Imply there is something between S & N. Need quote from J or S re

"double date." (2) Do S & N have a history? Maybe dated briefly in high school? Shoot a scene with J & S to discuss. (3) Scene with S & N. Gym?

Of course, Trevor had no idea whether Scarlett and Naveen had any history. Regardless, he knew it would be difficult to persuade Scarlett to film alone with Naveen. He would have to sell it to her as production needing a scene of two people talking about Jane and Caleb—and who knew them better than their best friends? And if all else failed . . . well, the "accidental" run-in always worked.

Someone knocked on his door. "Trevor?"

He closed his notebook and tucked it away in a drawer. "Yes?"

Madison walked in, looking less put together than usual in a pair of faded jeans, a pink hoodie, and minimal makeup. Trevor wondered whether she was feeling okay; maybe it was just another late night of partying? "Good morning! You're right on time," he greeted her, standing up.

"Thanks for meeting with me on such short notice. I . . . wanted to introduce you to somebody."

Trevor raised his eyebrows. "Oh? I thought it was just you and me today."

"Sorry. I know. It's just that . . . well, it's kinda important."

Madison stepped aside, and a young woman walked in. No, not just a young woman . . . one of the most stunning young women Trevor had ever seen. And that was saying a lot, considering his line of business.

Trevor studied her, scrutinizing every detail of her appearance, not as a guy checking out a girl (although no one would blame him for doing so) but as a producer checking out potential talent. She oozed sensuality, everything from her all-black outfit (leather skinnies, suede platform ankle boots, and a sheer, oversize T-shirt that showed off her slender yet voluptuous figure) to her features (big, brown eyes darkly rimmed with smoky eyeliner, full, lush, glossy lips, high cheekbones, and a sleek, shoulder-length platinum bob).

Madison spoke up. "Trevor, this is my little sister, Sophia."

"Your . . . sister?" Trevor did a double take. Hmm, okay, he could see a slight resemblance. Maybe. "Nice to meet you, Sophia," he said, extending his hand.

Sophia shook his hand, gazing at him with an expression that was at once seductive and contemptuous. How old was she? Seventeen, eighteen? She was too young to have adopted—and perfected—such a look. "Hey," she said in a low, throaty voice.

"Sophia, this is the guy I was telling you about. He's the producer of my show," Madison said.

My show? Trevor suppressed a smile. "Are you in town for a visit, Sophia?" he asked, indicating for the two girls to sit down.

"I was. But now I'm thinking of moving here, you know, permanently. L.A.'s pretty cool," Sophie replied, casting a quick sideways glance at Madison.

Madison nodded. "Yeah, she's staying with me for a while, until she finds her own place. That's what I wanted to talk to you about, Trevor. Do you think it would be okay if she lived with me? I mean, could she be on the show, or . . ." Her voice trailed off uncertainly.

Trevor leaned back in his chair and regarded Madison, then Sophia, all the while keeping his face neutral. This was a totally unexpected surprise—Madison wanting to add her sister to the show, a sister he never knew existed, a sister whose looks were sure to boost ratings (at least with the eighteen to thirty-five male viewership). It would also be helpful to have someone for Madison to recap scenes with other than Gaby.

But why now? Why hadn't Madison brought Sophia in to meet him before or at least mentioned the fact that she *had* a sister? Come to think of it, he didn't know a lot about her family or her background.

"Well, what do you think, Trevor?" Madison sounded anxious, on edge. What was up with her today?

"I think it's a great idea," Trevor said finally, and he could actually *see* Madison's entire body grow slack with relief. Had she seriously been worried that he wouldn't let Sophia be on the show? Sophia, on the other hand, looked less relieved than smug. Her mouth curled up in a scornful half grin as she sat back in her chair, throwing her shoulders back and displaying her assets more prominently. The girl was intriguing.

"Isn't this awesome, Sophia?" Madison said, turning to her sister. "We're gonna be on TV together!" Her voice cracked with tension.

"Yeah, awesome," Sophia replied, picking at her manicure. "Hey, Trev? How much am I gonna get paid? I'm assuming it's a lot, cuz when I used to do modeling they paid me, like, ten thousand dollars a day."

Madison shot Sophia a furious look. Sophia smirked at her. *Hmm, more intriguing by the minute.* Trevor wasn't positive, but he was pretty sure that Sophia had never modeled: She was a little too short, and a little too well-endowed, and besides, wouldn't he have heard of her or seen her somewhere if she commanded that kind of daily rate? So Sophia was a liar on top of everything else. And her dynamic with Madison was fascinating, too. Maybe there was a Season 2 story line there?

"Have you ever been on TV before, Sophia?" Trevor asked her.

Sophia shrugged, which Trevor took to mean no.

"Well, it's not a big deal. It's reality, so you just have to be yourself."

Sophia began playing with her bottom lip—was that a nervous habit, or a gesture she used to get a guy's attention?—then smirked at Madison again. "Be myself. Yeah, that's what Madison does. I'm sure I can do it, too."

Madison looked away.

Definitely intriguing, Trevor thought.

16

OR MAYBE YOU'RE JUST BEING DELUSIONAL, AS USUAL

"And . . . that is a wrap! You are *très, très belle, ma chérie!* I could take pictures of you forever!"

Scarlett smiled politely at the *Maxim* photographer, an overly energetic French guy named Maurice, as she rose up from the round, silk-comforter-covered bed. The view out the window of their hotel suite was stunning, although Scarlett was so exhausted from the nearly day-long shoot that she could barely appreciate it.

One of the nameless wardrobe assistants handed Scarlett a terry-cloth robe, which she slipped on over her "outfit": black lace La Perla lingerie and nude lace-up stilettos. Actually, this was one of *many* outfits she'd worn over the course of the shoot. First, they had shot her by the hotel pool in various bikinis (the stylist had let her pick her favorites from a rack of over fifty, all noticeably lacking in fabric on the back side) and a shocking amount of body oil. The second shot had taken place in one of the hotel's lounges, with Scarlett sitting at the bar . . . standing behind the bar making drinks . . . then actually stretched out *on* the bar. (She had insisted that they clean it, twice. She had been to enough bars to know that they weren't the most sanitary of places.)

Their last location had been the suite, rented for the day by *Maxim*. Scarlett had overheard her hairstylist saying to one of the assistants that the five-thousand-a-night room was often occupied by newly single male celebs needing a temporary residence. The fact that it was just upstairs from a club that was frequented by hot girls who liked male celebs, single or not, was a bonus. The hairstylist had added that one of her clients had moved in during a nasty divorce and liked it so much he stayed for nearly a year. (Scarlett hoped it was at a discount.)

When they first got up to the suite, the *Maxim* art director had explained to Scarlett that they wanted two shots there: one on the bed and one in the glass shower with the door all steamed up. Bed? Glass shower?

Scarlett had immediately turned to the PopTV publicist, Melissa, who had not said anything to her before about beds or showers; in fact, when Melissa originally told Scarlett about the *Maxim* gig, she said something about a "classy shoot" that showed off Scarlett's "natural beauty," and how it was all a "great opportunity" to get Scarlett "out there."

Okay, so maybe Scarlett had promised to have a better attitude about PopTV and *L.A. Candy.* But she wasn't an idiot, and she wished everyone would stop treating her like one. There was nothing "classy" about posing on a bed or in the shower. (The shower photo, "the most important one of the day" according to the *Maxim* art director, was going to stretch across the first two pages of the article with HOT CANDY or some similar title imposed on the steamed-up glass.) And there was nothing "natural" about two inches of padding in one's bra cups. Obviously, PopTV had wanted the August cover for Scarlett because it was going to increase their show's male viewership, and most guys weren't too interested in classy or natural.

Scarlett had eventually agreed to the bed shot but not the shower shot. Aside from Liam and the rubber ducky next to her tub, no one was gonna see her like that, soaping up. Melissa, Maurice, the *Maxim* art director, the stylist, and a few others from the magazine on set gathered around to discuss what to do. Thirty minutes, four phone calls, and one bagel (snatched from Scarlett's hand by Melissa: "Eat *after* the shoot") later, the shower shot was killed.

And now the bed shot was done. Finally. Scarlett said a hasty good-bye to everyone, thanked Maurice, and went to change. She was cooking dinner for Liam tonight, and she couldn't wait. Not the cooking-dinner part—her culinary skills had not magically improved since she and Jane had Caleb and Naveen over last week—but the Liam part. She hadn't seen him in days, due to their busy schedules, and she missed him big-time.

Unfortunately, she was also long overdue to have a

conversation with him about . . . well, recent events. She *wasn't* looking forward to that part of the evening.

On her way out of the hotel, she saw a familiar figure sitting in the lobby, scrolling through her phone. A familiar, unwelcome figure. Should she try to sneak by and avoid a confrontation, or . . .

"Scarlett? What are *you* doing here?"

Scarlett sighed. No escape. "Hey, Madison. So nice to see you, too. I could ask you the same thing."

"I have a meeting. *Maxim* is doing a shoot here today, and it was the only time I had in my schedule. I'm talking to one of the editors about doing the August cover," Madison said smugly.

"Oh, really? That's funny, because I just finished the shoot . . . for the August cover."

Madison's eyes blazed. "What? What are you talking about? The girl from the PopTV press department definitely said August."

"Maybe she got it wrong," Scarlett suggested. *Or maybe you're just being delusional, as usual,* she thought.

"Look, this is *my* cover, and you're trying to steal it from me!" Madison said angrily.

A young woman standing nearby was looking at them with a little too much interest. That's all Scarlett needed, for some eavesdropping stranger to call the tabloids with a hot tip about the two of them arguing over the stupid August cover.

Scarlett fake-smiled, shifting gears. "I'm soooo late for

a dinner date," she told Madison apologetically. "I'll catch you later, okay? Good luck with your meeting!"

With that, Scarlett turned and rushed out the door, trying not to laugh at the stunned expression on Madison's face, and savored her tiny victory.

"Hey, these fish tacos are great! I thought you said you didn't know how to cook." Liam was seated next to Scarlett at her apartment, scarfing down the tacos she had just made.

"I don't. This is all I know how to make. And the main ingredient was in the freezer twenty minutes ago," Scarlett said, secretly pleased.

Liam grinned and leaned over to kiss her on the cheek. "I've missed you," he said.

"I've missed you, too. I wish the semester was over already, and we could spend more time together."

"That's, like, in a month, right?" Liam said, taking another bite of his taco.

"Yeah, I'm counting the seconds."

"I'm gonna teach you how to wakeboard this summer."

"Wrong, Ferguson! I'm gonna teach *you* how to wakeboard this summer."

Liam laughed, then kissed her again, this time on the lips. Scarlett twined her fingers through his long, light brown wavy hair, then pulled him closer. She had wanted to prepare him a special dinner, complete with candles, wine, and romantic music in the background. It was a little cheesy for her taste, but she wanted to make up for being so MIA lately. (Jane was out with Caleb, so they had the place to themselves.) And to put him in a relaxed, happy mood before she had The Talk with him about Naveen.

She had been avoiding the issue for a while, and she really couldn't put it off any longer. For one thing, she knew that the episode featuring the Caleb-Naveen dinner party (as well as Jane and Caleb's official "first date" at some fancy Italian restaurant) was airing next week. After it aired, the blogs would be buzzing with insane headlines like: THE NEW BOYS OF *L.A. CANDY* and SCARLETT'S NEW MAN?

But more important, one of the big tabloids had hit the stands this morning with a trashy piece about Scarlett and Naveen filming together, going on dinner dates, and becoming an item—compliments of a "source close to Scarlett." WTF? Where did reporters *get* this crap? Liam apparently hadn't seen the article yet, judging from his pleasant mood tonight. But she couldn't exactly keep him away from magazine stands, bookstores, grocery store aisles, and the internet.

"Soooo." Scarlett sat back in her chair and began fiddling with her napkin. *Just get it over with,* she told herself. "You remember those two guys Janie and I know from high school? Caleb and Naveen?"

"Yeah. I mean, I've never met them. But I saw their pictures in a magazine at my dentist's office, remember?" Liam said wryly.

"Um, right." *Add "dentist's offices" to the list,* Scarlett thought. "Well, I wanted to tell you . . . that is . . . Trevor kind of made us invite them over for dinner last week," Scarlett blurted out.

Liam frowned. "I don't get it."

"Trevor said he wants us to hang out on camera as a foursome because there needs to be guys on the show," Scarlett babbled on. "He said it's not good for ratings that Jane isn't dating anybody, and I'm dating you, except you can't be on the show, so as far as the public is concerned, I'm not dating anybody, either. Except now Janie *is* dating Caleb." She didn't stop to voice her opinion on the subject, namely, that she wasn't thrilled, and she hoped her best friend wasn't going to get hurt—*again.* "That's going to be on the next episode. And so is the dinner party with the four of us. And I just wanted to let you know that dinner party was totally innocent . . . well, except when Jane and Caleb started making out in the kitchen. But Naveen and I are friends from a long time ago, and you know that Trevor is always looking for a story. It's just, you never know how Trevor's gonna edit stuff, right? And then this crazy article came out today, but it's all made up, and—"

"Wait, what?" Liam put his fork down and pushed his plate away. "*What* article?"

"One of the tabloids lied and said Naveen and I hooked up," Scarlett explained. Was it her imagination, or was she talking really, really fast? "Which we never did! I mean, not *never*, because we did kind of have a thing in high

147

school. But it was *high school*, and it only happened once. Now we're just friends. I mean, we're *barely* friends. We're only hanging out because Trevor is making us." She leaned closer and gazed into Liam's blue eyes. "You understand, right? This is my job, and it's not like I'm choosing to hang out with these guys."

She stopped and took a deep breath, waiting for Liam to nod sympathetically and tell her that he understood completely. But he was looking at her with a weird, tense expression and not saying a word.

"What? Say something. You're not mad at me, are you?" Scarlett said.

Liam sighed. "No, I'm not mad at you, Scarlett. But you should have told me this stuff before. And yeah, I get that this is your job. But do you have to pretend you're dating this guy for the show?"

"I'm not! Trevor just wants us to hang out, that's all."

"Yeah, well, what does that mean, 'hang out'? What does *Trevor* mean by that?"

"I have no idea what goes on in Trevor's mind. Well, maybe I do, but I'd rather not think about it. The point is . . . I'm not Trevor's puppet. He can't make me do stuff I don't want to do. And I absolutely, positively don't want to even *pretend* to date Naveen. I want to date *you*. I *am* dating you."

Liam regarded her silently.

Scarlett grabbed his hand. "In a perverse, mixed-up kind of way, maybe it's a *good* thing that Trevor's into his make-believe head games about me and Naveen. Maybe this way, he won't give me a hard time about dating you."

"He's giving you a hard time about that? Still?"

Scarlett shrugged. "He's not happy that I'm dating someone who can't be filmed. It was the same thing with Jane and Braden. Not that they were dating, exactly. But you know what I mean."

"I guess? God, this show is really messed up."

"Yeah, I know. But it's a job. A good job with serious money. And I'm lucky to have it." When Liam gave her a strange look, Scarlett quickly added, "I wasn't saying that because you don't have a . . . I mean, I need the money to pay for tuition so I don't have to freeload off my parents. And someday, after I graduate, I'll have a way better job where I won't feel like I'm living in a fish bowl. I mean, you *know* this is totally twisted, right? There's my *real* life, like tonight. Then there's my *other* life, in front of the cameras. And then there's my *third* life, after Trevor's done editing my scenes and they air on TV."

Liam cracked a smile. "Yeah, that's twisted, all right."

Scarlett leaned over and hugged him. Liam hugged her back. Good. He was okay. Things were going to be okay between them.

"I'm gonna change the music. What is this? You getting sappy on me?" Liam said after a moment, extricating himself from their hug and walking over to the CD player. He pulled a CD case off the shelf and studied it. Scarlett could tell that the subject of Naveen and Trevor and the rest of it was closed. Which was fine with her. "Hey, we're still on for this Saturday and Sunday, right? For your birthday surprise?"

"Yes, we are, sir," Scarlett said, digging into another taco. "What are we doing? Can you give me a tiny hint?"

"It's going to be amazing. Other than that, you're not getting a single hint, so don't even try." Liam pulled out a cream envelope peeking out from between two CDs. "What's this?"

"NOOOO!" Scarlett leapt to her feet and grabbed the envelope out of Liam's hands. He looked totally confused. "It's . . . um . . . it's a surprise I have for you! So you can't look, okay?"

"O-*kay*." Liam cocked his head. "What kind of surprise? My birthday's not till September, you know?"

"It's not a birthday surprise. It's a *different* kind of surprise. Just be patient, please? I promise I'll tell you soon."

"You'd better." Liam slid his arms around her waist and hugged her again. Scarlett crammed the envelope into the back pocket of her jeans as she nestled in closer, hugging him back. She couldn't believe he had come *this close* to seeing the return address on the envelope. She had hidden it on the CD shelf yesterday, quickly and carelessly (obviously), because it was on the coffee table and Jane had almost picked it up.

It was Scarlett's first acceptance letter, from Columbia University in New York City. She had danced a little victory dance around the apartment when she read it. Then grown very subdued when she realized that she had a choice now. She could leave USC this fall if she wanted to.

The problem was, she didn't want to leave Liam. Or Jane.

What was she going to do?

17

THE PERFECT GUY

As Jane drove out of the underground parking garage of her apartment building on Tuesday morning, she spotted four—no, *five*—cars pulling away from the curb. Paparazzi. The tinted windows and absence of plates were telltale signs, not to mention that these same five cars had been following her almost every day the past few weeks. She thought one of them might be the creep that had bumped her car from behind when she was on her way to meet up with Braden.

It was so odd . . . these men, whose names she didn't even know, followed her all day long. (And presumably the other *L.A. Candy* girls, too. Scarlett had been complaining bitterly about the ones tailing her around town.) They "accompanied" Jane when she went to work, dropped off her dry cleaning, shopped for groceries at Whole Foods—and of course, when she filmed. There seemed to be more and more of them at the PopTV shoots lately, particularly the outdoor shoots. Dana and Trevor were not happy about this for a couple of important reasons. First, the paparazzi often wandered into the frame and scenes had to be reshot. The PopTV crew got into frequent, sometimes violent arguments with the paps about this, and just last week, the network had to replace several expensive digital cameras that had been broken during a tussle in order to avoid a lawsuit. Second, the photos were sold to the tabloids, and they documented the girls' activities, outfits, and so forth in a slightly different, more accurate way than the show. Whereas Trevor took liberties with editing—say, patching together two scenes from a month apart into one "seamless" scene that pretended to take place on the same day—the gossip rags could print images of these events as they really happened. Magazines were getting more savvy about this sort of thing, as was the public. Which made Trevor and the other network execs extremely *tense*.

Jane continued driving down the street, stopped at the stop sign, and made a left. She watched in the rearview mirror as each of the five cars turned left behind her. Three of them didn't even bother to heed the stop sign. She was on her way to film a quick scene at a café in West Hollywood with Hannah, after which she had an eleven o'clock meeting at the office with Fiona (off camera), after which she had a lunch date with Caleb in Beverly Hills (on camera). She wasn't thrilled with the idea of showing up at the café shoot with a party of five—or more, since sometimes, there was more than one pap per car, or alternatively, once she showed up at a location with a group of them in tow, more would magically show up, easily doubling or tripling their number. Really, it was insane.

A few minutes later, Jane reached Sunset Boulevard. Since the incident en route to Braden's in late March, she had gotten savvier. She had learned through experience that making a bunch of quick turns didn't lose them; it simply made them drive more recklessly and ignore obstacles like red lights and pedestrians. She had also grown to appreciate stop-and-go traffic, especially on Sunset at this time of day. If she switched lanes at just the right moment, she could usually split herself off from a car or two that might be stuck in a slow line of vehicles. And if she could manage to get one or more of them in front of her, she could turn off onto a side street that they had already passed.

Using these methods, Jane managed to whittle down her "entourage" to one SUV by the time she reached the café and parked on the street. Unfortunately, she saw that there was a small group of paparazzi already waiting for her in front of the café. Just beyond them, she saw some PopTV crew members setting up, looking annoyed.

The cameras began flashing when Jane stepped out of her car, and soon she was surrounded.

"Jane!"

"Give us a smile!"

"Who are you meeting for breakfast, Jane?"

Oh, God. Jane took a deep breath, trying to calm her nerves. For her, paps in person were way worse than paps in cars. After all these months, she was still terrified of the sight of these grown men—*strangers*—running toward her, shouting at her, taking her picture. She wasn't sure she would ever get used to it. (After escaping them, she would often shake for five, ten minutes before she could calm down.)

"Jane!"

"Over here!"

"Who designed your dress, Jane?"

Jane realized she couldn't stand there all day like a trapped animal. She adjusted her sunglasses with a trembling hand and made her way through the gauntlet of paparazzi, pretending that this was all perfectly normal. Which it wasn't.

Luckily, there were no paparazzi waiting for her when she arrived at Villa Blanca at noon.

Gazing around the sunlight-filled dining room, Jane ran a hand across her black-and-white wrap dress, smoothing the microphone wire underneath. The PopTV camera guys were already in place, and only a few of the customers at the Beverly Hills restaurant seemed fazed by their presence. Maybe it was because the show filmed there often. Or maybe people in L.A. were just used to TV crews.

When Matt gave her the signal, Jane crossed the room to the corner table where Caleb sat waiting for her. She was excited to see him. New relationships always made her feel this way. (Even though theirs wasn't *technically* new.

And she hadn't been in a lot of relationships, new or otherwise.) This was their third date since last Thursday, all of them on camera, and with each one, she became more convinced that Caleb was the perfect guy for her at this point in her life. He was so easy to hang out with—no drama, no surprises, no stress. He was a total gentleman, too, like the way he was at the hospital week before last.

And he was really, really cute, which didn't hurt.

"Hey." He stood up and put his hand on her elbow, kissing her briefly on the lips. He smelled yummy, like woodsy aftershave.

"Hey. You look nice." Jane hadn't expected to see him wearing a navy linen blazer over his button-down shirt. He wasn't usually so dressed up and besides, hadn't he come straight from a construction site?

"Thanks. You're looking pretty gorgeous yourself."

"Thanks. Sorry I'm late. My eleven o'clock meeting ran over." Jane didn't add that it had started late because her café shoot had taken longer than expected, due to interference by the paparazzi.

"Yeah, I got your message. No worries. How'd it go?" Caleb pulled a chair out for her.

Jane sat down and tucked her bag under the table. "Good, I guess? There's so much going on. I feel like I'm working twenty-four/seven lately. I mean, Aja's engagement party is, like, a full-time project. *And* there's a video-game launch at Playground the day after tomorrow, and a restaurant opening next Tuesday. Oh, and

Scar's birthday party this Saturday! You're coming to that, right?"

"Wouldn't miss it."

"Great!"

The waitress came by to take their orders. "The chopped salad, please, and an iced tea," Jane said, glancing at the menu.

"The filet mignon, medium rare. And a Sam Adams," Caleb said.

"Steak? Wow, you must be hungry," Jane teased him.

"Hey, don't give me a hard time. I've been hauling steel beams all week," Caleb said with a grin.

"When's that house going to be finished?"

"Hopefully by the end of May? The family's been living in a one-bedroom apartment for the last two years . . . and there's five of them. So they're pretty excited."

"Wow, I'm sure."

The waitress came back with their drinks. Caleb picked up his beer and glanced around. "Nice place. Guess the owner likes white."

"Well it *is* called *Villa Blanca.*"

"*Blanca.* White. Got it."

"Hey, speaking of . . . remember the Valentine's Day dance, senior year? I wore that white dress I bought at Forever 21, and—"

"Oh, yeah, the super-short one. You looked hot in that," Caleb cut in.

Jane blushed. "Caleb! It wasn't *that* short. Anyway . . .

you were trying to dance to that Soulja Boy song, and you kind of spazzed and ended up spilling punch all over my dress."

"I did *not* spaz. Jenn Nussbaum bumped into me," Caleb said, pretending to be hurt.

Jane laughed. "Maybe. Or maybe she was just trying to get close, cuz she had a huge crush on you."

"She did not."

"She absolutely did, and you know it. Half the girls at the school had a crush on you."

"Well, I didn't notice, cuz *you're* the only girl *I* had a crush on."

He reached across the table and squeezed her hand. Jane smiled and dropped her gaze. It was true; Caleb used to be one of the most desirable guys at their school. For a long time after they began dating, she used to wonder, *Why me? There are so many girls who are prettier.* Self-esteem wasn't exactly one of Jane's strong suits. Over the years, Scar had tried to get her to stop being so hard on herself. And it was working. Kind of. Slowly, gradually, Jane was starting to feel better about herself, more confident.

She lifted her gaze and stared into Caleb's chocolate brown eyes and thought, *I deserve a sweet, smart, handsome guy like you, who likes me for who I am.*

The image of Braden flitted through her mind. Braden *might* have been the perfect guy for her . . . if only he had given her some indication that he cared about her that way. *Oh, well. Too late, Braden James . . .*

158

"What are you thinking about?" Caleb asked her. "Looks kinda intense, whatever it is."

Jane laced her fingers through his. "I'm just happy to be out with you."

"Yeah? Me too."

For the rest of the hour, Jane and Caleb continued to bring up funny memories from high school: Jane getting the hiccups during opening night of the drama club's *The Mousetrap* . . . Caleb accidentally kicking a soccer ball into the referee's face during a match (the ref was unhurt but *really* mad). As the waitress cleared their plates, Jane glanced at her watch and realized that it was after one o'clock.

"I'm sorry, I've gotta go," Jane said apologetically. "I have a meeting at two."

"Yeah, I've gotta go, too. Those steel beams are calling out to me."

"Jane! Caleb!"

Dana was approaching their table. "Change of plans. We're not gonna film your exit, because there are, like, two dozen paparazzi out there," she explained.

Them again? Jane frowned. They were in rare form today.

"We tried to talk to them, but they won't go away," Dana went on. "So. You can take off your mike packs now, and Jane . . . we'll see you tomorrow for your scene with Scarlett, and then Thursday at Playground. Caleb, you'll be there, too, right?"

"Absolutely."

"Good. Bye, you two. Nice job today."

Jane and Caleb extracted their mike packs and handed them to one of the sound guys. As Jane rose to go, she said, "Hey, Caleb? Since there are so many photographers outside, we should probably leave separately. You want to go first, and I'll go a few minutes after? Better yet, I'll see if the restaurant will let us leave out the back."

"Wait. Why?" Caleb asked her, running a hand through his hair. "Aren't we supposed to be photographed together and stuff? It's good publicity for the show, right?"

"Yeah, but . . . it's gonna be a zoo out there, and I don't want to be late for my meeting. Besides, they were all over us at La Dolce Vita last Thursday and at the *Makeover* premiere last night." Not to mention the fact that they were all over her at the café earlier. Enough was enough.

Caleb shrugged. "I guess. Whatever."

Jane hooked her arm through his. Was it her imagination, or did he seem a little annoyed? "I'm gonna talk to the maître d' about letting me go out the back. You wanna come with me?"

"No, you go on ahead. I'm gonna go out front so I can have the valet get my car."

As they kissed good-bye, Jane had the sudden, weird feeling that Caleb actually *liked* being photographed by paparazzi. What was up with that?

18

KIND OF THE TRUTH

"Sophia . . . so I need you to ring the front doorbell when Matt gives you the okay," Trevor said. "Then, Madison . . . you're going to answer the door, and, Sophia, you're going to say: 'Surprise!' And, Madison, you're going to look surprised. Got it, girls?"

Madison fluffed her hair in the reflection of the hall mirror, then peered quickly at the brown leather notebook in Trevor's hands. What was he doing at her apartment, anyway, trying to direct the shoot? She was pretty sure they already had a director. Trevor tended to show up on the set when something important was going on, but he always stayed in the background, just observing. Why was today so special? Because they were filming Sophie's "surprise visit" to L.A.?

After their stressful (in Madison's opinion) meeting on Sunday, Trevor had asked her for some background information on Sophie, and Madison had offered him a plausible-sounding explanation (she'd worked on it for weeks) that Sophie was eighteen and had been crashing with some friends in New York City since graduating from high school last June. In turn, Trevor had semi-scripted a story about Sophie showing up unexpectedly in L.A. (which was kind of the truth, minus the blackmail part, *ha-ha*), and then deciding to stay for good (which was also kind of the truth, except that Madison would much rather see the little bitch go far, far away). This way, viewers could be introduced to Sophie, now "Sophia," on the show versus off screen; after all, she couldn't *not* be there one episode, then suddenly be there the next.

Sophie snaked her hand down her really, really low neckline. "These wires hurt like hell," she complained, in the process giving Trevor a bird's-eye view of practically everything. *Slut.* "Why do I have to wear a microphone, Trev? Can't I just say my lines super-loudly?"

"It doesn't work that way, Sophia," Trevor explained. "Don't worry, you'll get used to the mike pack."

"You are so mean!" Sophie whined in a little-girl voice. Then she smiled silkily, letting Trevor know that she was kidding. He smiled back.

"Soph . . . *Sophia*, let's just do this, okay?" Madison said, gritting her teeth. She wasn't sure how much more she could stomach of her sister's attention-whore behavior. Emphasis on "whore."

Sophie turned her gaze on Madison. The brown contacts were disconcerting; Madison was accustomed to seeing violet blue. In fact, when Sophie was a toddler, Madison used to tease her that her eyes were that color because she loved to eat blueberries so much.

"What's your hurry, Maddy? You got a hot date with your boyfriend? Derek, right?" Sophie said, batting her eyelashes.

Trevor frowned. "Madison, you have a boyfriend? Why didn't I know about this? Is he going to film?"

Madison clenched her fists and forced herself to take a deep breath. Was Sophie out of her *mind*? Did she want to ruin *everything*? Trevor would not be too understanding about one of his stars sleeping with—and being supported by—a married man. A married, much older man. And Sophie absolutely couldn't call her "Maddy," which was her old nickname from back home. "No, there's no boyfriend. Dirk, not Derek, was ages ago. I'm totally single these days. Which is how I like it," Madison told Trevor.

"Yeah? What about that dude, what's his name, back in Armpit Falls? You went out with him for, like, forever. Didn't seem like you loved being 'single' then," Sophie sneered.

"Did you say . . . Armpit Falls?" Trevor asked.

"It's a joke, Trevor. My sister's got a weird sense of humor. Can we get started? I have to be someplace in an hour," Madison lied, pretending to check her watch as she seethed silently. God! Did Sophie have no self-control whatsoever?

"Madison, I'm not sure we're going to be done in an

hour," Trevor pointed out. Now *he* looked annoyed.

"Not if we keep talking about my old boyfriends from a hundred years ago. Let's just get started, okay?"

As it turned out, the shoot took more than three hours, mostly because Sophie couldn't follow directions. (Surprise, surprise!) She also kept looking right at the camera and posing, instead of acting natural.

By the time they finally wrapped, Madison was ready for a strong drink and some retail therapy. Luckily, this scene with Sophie was the only one she had to shoot today.

"You did great," Trevor said to Sophie as he checked something on the monitor. *Liar,* Madison thought. Or was he just too mesmerized by Sophie's looks to tell her the truth? "So. I'll see both of you at the Playground party tomorrow night, right?"

"The Playground party?" Madison repeated. "What Playground party?"

Trevor stared at her. "Seriously, Madison? I'm talking about the video-game launch party you've been helping Jane and Hannah plan at work."

"Oh, *that* Playground party," Madison said. She had totally forgotten about it, and besides, she hadn't done much in the way of "helping" Jane and Hannah. She mostly just showed up at the office whenever the PopTV cameras were filming. It wasn't like Fiona expected her to come into the office to *work.* "Of course I'll be there. Sophia and I can drive over together."

"Perfect. And make sure to check in with Dana before

she leaves today." Dana was across the living room, talking to Matt. "She'll have some instructions for you about what time to arrive and so forth." Trevor turned to Sophie. "Sophia, this is the first time you'll be meeting the rest of the *L.A. Candy* girls. We haven't told any of them that Madison has a sister, so they should all be a little surprised. I can fill you in about that tomorrow."

"Is Gaby back?" Madison said. She hadn't heard from her in weeks. "When did she—"

"So what do you want me to wear for the party, Trev?" Sophie interrupted, studying her nails. "Do I need to wear, like, a dress?"

"Madison can help you with that," he told her. "I'm sure you're aware that shopping is one of your sister's finest skills."

Sophie grinned. "Awesome. I'll let you buy me a new dress, Maddy. You know, as a 'welcome to L.A.' present or whatever."

"Wait, why don't we get some cameras on that?" Trevor suggested. "Dana! What's on the schedule for this afternoon? Do you think we could clear one of the usual stores we shoot at?" he called out.

Sophie smirked at Madison. *Bitch,* Madison thought. *Like I'm buying you anything.*

But Madison knew that she would probably have no choice. Although it would be a bit of a challenge, since her credit cards were nearly maxed out. Knowing Sophie, she would pick out the most expensive outfit she could find, just to piss Madison off. And knowing Trevor, he would spin an entire episode out of the two girls arguing over price tags, in essence turning Madison into the smarter, more responsible sister (the "boring" one) and Sophie into the wilder, more impulsive sister (the "fun" one). Ugh.

I'm trapped, Madison thought angrily. She was stuck with Sophie, trying to keep her happy and also keep her from revealing Madison's many secrets, until Sophie got whatever she wanted out of the *L.A. Candy* deal (fame, fortune, a rich boyfriend?) and then . . . *what*? Moved to Australia? Left Madison alone forever? Not likely. In the meantime, Madison was going to have to figure out how to rein Sophie in and regain the upper hand.

But how?

19

SHE SAID, SHE SAID

Jane adjusted her earpiece and scanned the main room of Playground, mentally double-checking everything. There were several large flat-screens on the walls, and remote controls were available at each table so that the guests could try out the new Knife Assassin's Revenge video game. In actuality, the remotes were there so that photographers could take pictures of celebrities in minidresses holding them . . . and gamers at home would see these pictures that combined their two favorite things (i.e., a hot girl and a violent video game) and immediately buy the game.

The Knife Assassin's Revenge logo was everywhere: on signs, posters, even on the cocktail napkins. Jane nodded, satisfied. She and Hannah had worked overtime to get every last detail of this party perfect. Madison, who was supposed to help out, had done the opposite, distracting everyone with her on-camera drama. But it didn't matter now. Jane and Hannah had somehow pulled it all together, and it was going to be an amazing night.

"Guests are starting to arrive." Hannah's voice crackled over the earpiece. "Oliver's checking people through. Oh, and guess what? The Marley twins' publicist just called and said they're coming!"

"Ohmigod, awesome!" Jane said. The celebrity head count was really starting to add up. "Oh . . . hey . . . can you make sure that my friend Caleb Hunt is on the list? I think I put his name on, but it's been so crazy. Oh, and Naveen Singh, too."

"Your boyfriend and his friend? No problem," Hannah said, giggling.

"He's not my boyfriend! I mean, we just started dating again." Jane wasn't sure she was ready to call Caleb that in front of the entire world just yet. She was glad that the PopTV cameras were still setting up and that she hadn't been miked yet. She hoped Hannah hadn't been miked yet, either. "Speaking of boyfriends . . . yours has been really helpful with this party. That DJ he recommended is awesome."

"Yeah, right? We should definitely use her in the future."

Jane noticed that Hannah *didn't* say, *He's not my boyfriend!* about Oliver. Things were obviously getting serious between them. Jane was happy for Hannah. She didn't know a lot about Oliver, except that he was a communications major at UCLA and loved dogs (which in Jane's opinion was an asset in any guy). *And* he was super-nice and good at his job.

As Jane talked to Hannah, her gaze fell on a bare table across the room . . . a table that was supposed to be piled high with small black-and-silver totes. *Crap!* Where were the gift bags? "Is Madison here yet?" she asked Hannah.

"I haven't seen her. She was supposed to bring the gift bags, wasn't she?"

"Yeah. I'd better . . . no, can *you* call her on her cell and see where the hell she is?"

"I'm on it!"

Hannah signed off. Just then, someone touched Jane's arm. "Um, excuse me? Aren't you that actress from that show? I looooove you so much!" said a high-pitched voice.

Jane turned around, wondering what strange fan was stalking her now . . . but it was just Scar, munching on a celery stick. With her were Deb Rafferty, their trainer from the gym, and a familiar-looking brunette.

"Ha-ha, very funny, Scar," Jane said, giving her a quick hug. She smiled at Deb. "Hey, how are you? I'm sorry I had to cancel today. Things were kind of nuts."

"No worries, we'll just go twice as hard tomorrow to make up for it," Deb joked.

"This is my friend Chelsea, from school," Scarlett said, indicating the brunette. "She's super-smart, so make sure you use really big words when you talk to her."

Chelsea playfully hit Scarlett on the arm. "Stop it, Scarlett."

Dana approached the group, waving her clipboard in

the air. "Jane! Scarlett! You need to get miked right now! We have to film your entrances before too many people show up," she said, fidgeting with her earpiece. "Deb and Chelsea, right? I need you two to see Alli—that's the girl over there in the black shirt—so you can sign releases and get miked, too."

Deb and Chelsea took off, and one of the sound guys came by with a couple of packs for Jane and Scarlett. Jane noticed Trevor near the bar (talking to that awful editor from *Gossip* magazine, Veronica Bliss, and some woman in a leopard-print dress) and wondered: Was Trevor here tonight as a guest or producer—or a little of both?

As Jane and Scarlett slid their respective mike packs under their clothes, Dana said, "So you guys know Gaby's back from her vacation, right? She should be here any minute. She might already be on the red carpet. Anyway . . . when you see her, don't say anything, okay?"

"Say anything about what?" Jane said, confused. Scarlett *had* mentioned that Gaby looked different the last time she saw her, kind of like a mini-Madison, which was not good.

"Just keep the comments general, like 'I like your dress' or whatever. What, Ramon?" Dana barked into her headset. "Gaby's here? Good. What do you mean, we're short one camera? Can't they . . . fine, I'm coming now." She hurried away.

Jane and Scarlett exchanged a look. What was up with Dana tonight? She seemed even more frazzled than usual.

"Jane? Are you there?" It was Hannah again, on the earpiece. "I can't reach Madison. But Isaac was still at the office, and he's driving over with the gift bags right now. He'll be here in ten minutes."

"Good. Thanks." Jane turned back to Scarlett and smiled. "Sorry, it's probably going to be crazy like this the whole night."

"No worries, I know you're working," Scarlett said.

"What's Liam up to tonight?"

"He's out of town. He has this freelance gig in San Francisco all week."

So. That explained why Jane hadn't heard from Liam about Scarlett's surprise birthday party. Not that he necessarily would have contacted her about it, but still. Now, she was doubly glad she was planning the party, since Scar would have something fabulous to do on her big day. Of course, Scar wasn't one to fuss over her birthday—she usually preferred something totally last-minute and casual with Jane and whatever other friends happened to be around. But this year would be an exception.

"Is Caleb here?" Scarlett asked her, glancing around.

"Not yet. He texted me and said he and Naveen are on their way."

Scar didn't reply. Jane hoped that Scar wouldn't feel too uncomfortable seeing Naveen tonight. She knew it was awkward for Scar to have to hang out with him on camera, since Liam couldn't be on the show.

Jane also hoped that Scar wasn't going to be weird

about Caleb. Her only comment since the two of them started dating again had been, "If he hurts you again, so help me God, I will personally inflict him with severe bodily pain." Typical Scar. Jane had reassured her that she and Caleb were taking things slowly, and that she wasn't going to set herself up for that kind of heartbreak again.

Jane knew Scar wasn't exactly happy about the latest voice-overs Jane had recorded for the show, recapping previous episodes for viewers and hinting at what was to come next. Jane wasn't thrilled about them, either. She didn't like having to say stuff like *I didn't think I was ready to start dating again after Jesse and I broke up. But now I can't stop thinking about Caleb.* Or: *It looks like MY best friend and Caleb's best friend can't stop thinking about each other, either. I wonder if they're going to hook up?* She had argued with Trevor about these lines, especially the ones about Scar and Naveen, but in the end, he had managed to persuade her to record them with no changes. "They're not supposed to be the truth, Jane," he had explained in his annoyingly calm voice. "They're supposed to make viewers want to watch the episode." Whatever.

Jane saw Dana signaling to her and Scar from the red carpet area. "Hey, we'd better get out front," she suggested.

"Sure. Let's get this over with," Scarlett agreed.

As they threaded their way through the room, Jane saw that the place was already starting to fill with guests (including D—she made a mental note to say hi to him later). The DJ was playing Lady Gaga . . . the barely clothed waitresses were beginning to seat people and serve drinks . . . and a small group was already checking out the video game, which looked pretty intense up there on the big screens. Good. Except for the gift bag snafu, which was now under control, everything was going perfectly and according to plan.

She and Scarlett neared the red carpet area, where people were waiting to walk the press line of photographers and reporters. Then Jane's gaze wandered to the end of the line, to a girl in a skintight black minidress on the arm of a really cute guy. Jane recognized the guy; he was Topher Gant, the super-hot young actor from a super-hot TV show called *My Town*. She didn't remember his name being on the guest list, although it was a huge coup having him here. And she felt like she'd met the girl before . . .

Jane grabbed Scarlett's arm. "Wait. Is that Gaby?" she whispered.

"Ohmigod!" Scarlett whispered back. "I think that's her? Except, um, when did she get double Ds?"

"Padded bra?" Jane guessed, not taking her eyes off Gaby.

Scarlett looked doubtful. "Or maybe she wasn't actually 'on vacation' these last few weeks. Maybe she was recovering. I've gotta say, the most I've ever come back from Mexico with was a tan. Oh, and a henna tattoo, once."

"No way!" Jane couldn't believe Gaby thought she needed plastic surgery. Gaby fussed over her appearance, sure, but she had always been kind of understated, even conservative, preferring her blouses buttoned almost to the top and her skirts just above the knees.

Gaby spotted the two girls and pranced up to them. "What an awesome party! Topher, these are my friends Jane and Scarlett."

"Hey," Topher said. His gorgeous blue eyes fixed briefly on Jane and Scarlett before cutting away, no doubt to see if there were more attractive/interesting/important people for him to talk to.

"Topher's an actor," Gaby explained. "He's on that new show *This Town*."

"*My Town*," Topher corrected her, sounding annoyed. "Where's the bar?"

"Over there," Jane said, pointing. "Gaby, I . . . uh . . . like your dress."

"Thanks! It's a Mario Nuñez."

Jane couldn't get over Gaby's transformation. It was clear from her bulging cleavage that she *had* had a procedure done. Combined with her heavy makeup, plumped lips, spray tan, slight weight loss, and obvious hair extensions, she looked like an oversize Barbie doll. It was more cartoonish than cute.

So *this* was what Dana had meant when she asked them not to say anything to Gaby. Jane knew there would be no explanation on the show as to why Gaby looked totally different. *L.A. Candy* was about the real lives of regular girls, and regular girls like Gaby didn't get boob jobs and lip injections. Or if they did, they didn't talk about it.

"So I just got back from vacation," Gaby spoke up, plucking an icy shot glass from a passing waitress's tray. "What'd I miss while I was gone?"

"Not much. Deb's got me doing a new Pilates routine at the gym. It's awesome," Scarlett replied.

"And I've been super-busy with work," Jane added.

Gaby blinked at Jane. "Oh, yeah. Speaking of . . . you should stop being so mean to Madison at the office! She said she comes up with all these amazing ideas, and you just blow them off! You should give her a chance."

Jane gaped at Gaby. Where had *that* come from? "Yeah, well, Fiona makes the final decisions about everything, anyway," she said as casually as she could manage. "Soooo. How was Mexico?" she said, hoping to change the subject.

"Madison's really upset, Jane. You should take her out to lunch and make up," Gaby persisted. "It's the least you could do. I mean, after everything you put her through."

"Everything *I* put her through?" Jane demanded.

Scar shot Jane a *not now* look. Jane took a deep breath and made herself mentally count to ten. She had no idea what sort of game Gaby was playing, or who was making her say these idiotic things (Trevor? Dana?). But Scar was right; Jane couldn't continue with this she-said, she-said drama without the risk of appearing as dysfunctional as Madison. She would have to have a private conversation with Gaby later, off camera.

Gaby blinked at Scarlett. "You should apologize to Madison, too. She was soooo depressed after you told

Jane all those rumors about her and Jane moved out of her apartment."

"What? Gaby, are you *on* something?" Scarlett blurted out.

"*Scar!*" Jane hissed. Now it was her turn to shut Scar up. "Hey, why don't we all get a drink before I have to start working? I think—"

"*O-M-G!* Is this a reunion or what?"

Uh-oh, Jane thought.

Madison sauntered up to the three girls, dressed in a tangerine minidress and black patent leather heels. "I hope you weren't talking about me," she trilled.

"Actually, we were," Gaby replied, air-kissing Madison. "Wow, you look hot!"

Jane started to mentally count to ten again, but only got up to three. "Madison, where have you been? You forgot about the gift bags!"

"Jane, you always stress about the details. It's no biggie—I'll send one of the intern boys over for them. Anyway, that's so not important right now. I want you guys to meet someone."

Jane noticed a girl standing directly behind Madison. She couldn't place her, although there was something eerily familiar about her. She was eighteen-ish, blond, and stunning. Jane was surprised that Madison would hang out with a friend—especially on camera—who so clearly outshined her in the looks department.

"Oooh, are you a model?" Gaby asked the girl.

The girl smiled and shrugged.

"Guys, this is my baby sister, Sophia," Madison announced.

Madison's . . . *sister*? Jane had no idea Madison even *had* a sister. Trevor had gone out and hired a friend for Jane; was it possible he'd cast a "sister" for Madison? She knew his definition of "reality" was sketchy at best, but the possibility seemed a little extreme, even for him.

"She's gonna be staying with me for a while," Madison went on.

"Oooh, fun!" Gaby said eagerly.

"Good thing you have a big apartment," was all Scarlett said.

Jane glanced curiously at Madison, then at Sophia, then at Madison again. Madison had a big, fake smile plastered on her face, as usual, but the expression in her eyes was troubled, almost pained. Jane had never seen Madison look like that before.

Something weird was going on. Was Madison unhappy about her (way prettier) sister sharing airtime with her? Or was it something else altogether?

20

GOSSIP FEST

"Can you believe this night?" Scarlett leaned back in the passenger seat of Jane's Jetta and put her bare feet up on the dashboard. Her laid-back demeanor was at odds with the seven-hundred-dollar dress that she was wearing on loan from some new designer. The cool April breeze blowing through the half-open windows felt great, especially after standing around in a jam-packed club all night. Scarlett was beyond tired but at the same time newly energized, because she was finally alone with her best friend . . . unmiked . . . and brimming with important topics to discuss.

"So where do we start? Sophia or Gaby?" Jane said. She, too, seemed ready for a marathon gossip fest.

"You mean, the crazy person posing as Gaby? Cuz that girl is definitely *not* Gaby."

"Do you think Madison brainwashed her? Or Trevor? Or both?"

"I think it might be her new publicist, Annabelle. She was at the party tonight. Short, curly brown hair, leopard-print dress. She was hovering over Gaby like a mother hen."

"Oh! Annabelle Weiss. I saw her name on the guest list. Ohmigod, I told Gaby to sign with her, didn't I?"

"Yep."

"God. Well, anyway . . . I noticed Annabelle talking to Trevor a lot. And Veronica Bliss. And she was hanging around Topher Gant, too. Hey, I wonder if she's also *his* publicist? And maybe she arranged for him and Gaby to come to the party together? I heard publicists do that, to make sure their clients get into the magazines."

Scarlett frowned. "You mean, like, fake that two people are dating so they'll get more press coverage?"

"I guess?"

"Ew."

Although . . . Scarlett realized that Trevor was doing something similar with her and Naveen (who was at the party tonight and who Dana kept ordering her to talk to). And that Scarlett was allowing it to happen. So what, exactly, did that say about her?

They passed the intersection of Sunset and La Cienega, and Scarlett was startled to see a gigantic image of herself on a billboard, wearing a hot pink bikini and lying on a gigantic Photoshopped bed of peppermint candies. The line WHO'S *YOUR* FAVORITE FLAVOR? was spelled out across the bottom in huge red letters. Classy. It was part of PopTV's new ad campaign, with each of the four girls in a different-color bikini against a different candy-theme background . . . because the ratings weren't high enough already?

"Seriously, I can't believe what a bitch Gaby was to us tonight," Scarlett mused out loud. "I'm definitely gonna have to have a little talk with her ASAP."

Jane nodded. "Me too."

"And what's up with Madison? She looked pretty stressed about having her 'baby sister' around."

"Yeah, I'm soooo glad *my* baby sisters aren't like Sophia," Jane agreed. "She was like Madison two-point-oh. Hopefully she's not here for long!"

Sophia had been quite a terror at the party, slamming back shots and flirting with anything with a heartbeat. Madison had stayed glued to her side all night, whispering furiously in her ear, no doubt telling her to cut it out. Which didn't seem to work too well.

"Sophia's proof that Caleb's not a cheater, though," Jane added.

"Come again?"

"He didn't even look her way when she made the moves on him. *Twice.* He didn't seem to notice Gaby's new, uh, assets, either. I'm just saying."

"Hmm."

Scarlett knew that after their breakup, Jane had wondered if Caleb might have been cheating on her at Yale. Which, in Scarlett's humble opinion, was a very likely scenario. Although maybe he had changed since then? "How are things going between you two, anyway? Are you guys in love again, or what?" Scarlett said, hoping that the answer was no.

"Who said I'm looking to fall in love? I just want a nice, stress-free relationship for a change."

"So you're happy?" Scarlett asked, hiding her *oh really?* expression. Because, really? She doubted Jane was able to be with a guy she truly liked and *not* fall in love.

"Definitely! Caleb is exactly what I need right now. It's just low-key with him, no pressure. Like tonight. See how I'm going home with you instead of with him? We're not like one of those clingy couples that need to be together twenty-four/seven."

Scarlett laughed. "Hey, watch it. It just so happens that I'm a real catch. And if Liam wasn't out of town, I would so stand you up for him."

"Ha-ha."

"So what does Braden think about you dating Caleb?"

"Braden? Um . . . well . . . I haven't mentioned it to him."

Scarlett raised an eyebrow. "Oh? Aren't you guys in touch? I mean, have you heard from him since he took off for Alaska or wherever?"

"Banff. Yeah, he emails a couple of times a week, but . . ." Jane's voice trailed off uncertainly.

Scarlett turned and stared at Jane, who was driving with one hand and twirling her hair with the other. Hmm.

Jane was obviously still hung up on Braden. Which might be the *real* reason why she wasn't madly in love with Caleb?

"Janie, have you ever told Braden how you feel about him?" Scarlett asked her gently.

"What? I spent the night with him! I think that's pretty clear."

"Okay. First of all, I've hooked up with plenty of guys that I didn't have feelings for. Sometimes hooking up is just hooking up, ya know? You can't expect Braden to read your mind."

Jane seemed to consider this. "Well, what if that's just it?" she said after a moment. "What if he just hooked up with me and doesn't actually have feelings for me?"

"Yeah, he doesn't care about you, Janie. That's why after losing his best friend and having the media drag his name through the mud, all because of you, the guy is still sending you emails twice a week."

"Whatever. I don't want to think about him anymore."

Scarlett laughed. "Right. Like I believe that. I think you and Braden need to get really, really drunk and confess your true feelings for each other."

Jane grinned. "Yeah, that sounds like a healthy start to a relationship. Besides, why are you saying this stuff about Braden? I thought you didn't like him."

"I like him fine, except for his commitment issues."

"Commitment issues?" Jane started twirling her hair again.

"You mean that girl he was stringing along for, like,

three years didn't clue you in? Willow, right?" Scarlett shook her head. "See, Janie, there are two types of guys who won't commit. The first type avoids relationships until he falls in love for real, and then he's yours forever. The second type avoids relationships, *period*. That's the type you want to stay far away from. The question is, which type is Braden?"

"I don't know, Dr. Phil," Jane joked. "Or should I say Dr. Harp? Has your mom been giving you therapy lessons?" Scarlett's mother was a shrink.

"Hey, shut it! I'm just trying to help."

Of course, Scarlett knew something about commitment issues because she used to have them herself . . . until she met Liam.

She gazed out at the twinkling lights of the city against the dark sky, wondering where he was right this second. On the nights they didn't spend together, they usually talked before going to bed, just to say hi and talk about their day. Scarlett checked the dashboard clock: 11:23. Not *too* late. She could still call him when she got home.

Liam was due back on Saturday—her birthday. The plan was for him to pick her up at 7 p.m. that night, her bags packed for whatever surprise he had in store for her. She couldn't wait.

Scarlett normally didn't get worked up about birthdays. Her family had never been into traditions and celebrations, so she grew up not expecting much each April 24. Usually, Jane had to drag her out and force her to do *something*, even if it was just going out with a few friends. Although some years Jane went all out, like on Scarlett's sixteenth birthday, when she organized a barbecue at the beach, followed by a girls-only sleepover, followed by a spa day.

But this year . . . well, Scarlett was excited about whatever plans Liam had for her. Knowing him, they were sure to be awesome.

21

THE OTHER TEAM'S PLAYBOOK

"Miss Jane! You've outdone yourself. Our birthday girl is going to be soooo surprised," D said, typing briskly on his iPad. "Tell me—what juicy little lie did you come up with to get her here tonight?"

"Dana told her to come by here at six to shoot a quick pickup scene," Jane replied. She stood back and studied the HAPPY BIRTHDAY, SCARLETT! banner she had just strung across the doorway of Coco de Ville. "What do you think? Higher or lower? Hmm, should I have gotten green letters instead of blue? Maybe I should just take it down. . . ."

"The sign is perfect! Honey, stop stressing and give me something to write about for my blog," D ordered her, patting the chair next to him.

"Hey! Don't post anything until after she gets here. I don't want you to ruin the surprise. I mean it, D!"

Jane sat down, wishing she didn't feel so anxious. But there was still much to do for Scar's birthday party, which was in less than three—no, *two*—hours.

The inside of Coco de Ville looked strange to Jane in the daytime, brightly lit and almost completely vacant. The floors were swept, the bar was clean, the mismatched, patterned cushions were neatly lined up, and there was a quiet hush in the air. It was hard to imagine that in just a short while, the place would be packed with people—drinking, dancing, shouting over the music, and spilling their cocktails.

Across the room, the PopTV crew was shutting down to break for dinner before resuming the shoot once the party started. They had spent the afternoon filming scenes of Jane and Hannah putting up decorations, making last-minute changes to the menu with the kitchen staff, and going over the playlist with the DJ. Hannah had just left to pick up a poster at OfficeMax: a "best of" collage of photos of Scar spanning from childhood to the present. Getting the photos had not been an easy project, since unlike Jane's parents, Scarlett's parents were not big on taking family pictures.

D had stopped by around three to watch the shoot and get some notes for his blog. In the old days before D-Lish (i.e., two months ago), he might have been *in* the shoot as a friend of Jane's versus observing from the sidelines. But Jane knew Trevor would never allow that now. It would be too weird to have a journalist who blogged *about* the show to also be *on* the show, especially because D was becoming very well-known very quickly. In any case, it had been a while since they had hung out, and Jane was happy to spend some time with him, even if it *was* during "work hours."

"So, have you talked to your gorge ex lately?" D asked Jane. "I hear rehab is doing wonders for him. If he manages to stay sober, I might ask him out myself."

"Yeah, good luck with that. And no, I haven't talked to him."

Which wasn't exactly the truth. Jane thought about the email she'd gotten from Jesse just this morning:

Didn't take you long to find a new boyfriend, Jane. Guess you're as big a liar as you always were.

She'd started to write back, then figured, what good would it do? Jesse had obviously heard about her and Caleb, which would not have been difficult, since their relationship was all over the media. She wished now that she hadn't listened to Trevor's "advice." It had been stupid, lying to Jesse and making him think that he still had a chance with her.

D's voice interrupted her thoughts. "Soooo. Was it super-awkward seeing Jesse at the hospital?"

"Yeah. I hadn't seen him since we broke up, and—" Jane stopped suddenly and craned her neck to see what D was typing. "Don't you *dare* write about me and Jesse in your blog! It's totally off the record! Do you hear me, D?"

"Calm down, baby cakes! I would never!"

Jane sighed. She reached over and straightened his bow

tie, which was large, striped, and vintage. "It's so confusing with you these days. I mean, you're my friend I tell private stuff to, *plus* you're a blogger. Should I just keep my mouth shut?"

"Honey, the only thing I ever publish about you is that you're a sweet, beautiful, un-Botoxed gem in a shark-infested sea of fakes." D set aside his iPad. "Let's change the subject! How is your *new* man-friend?"

"Caleb? He's, um, fine."

"Fine?" D leaned back and narrowed his eyes at her. "That doesn't sound good, honey."

"No, no! Caleb's really cool! It's just that"—Jane hesitated—"we've been dating for a couple of weeks now. Less than that, even. At first it was a lot of fun, you know, talking about high school and catching up and stuff. But . . . well . . . I'm kinda starting to wonder about him."

"What do you mean?"

"Well . . . like last night? We finally had a date without the crew. I was looking forward to seeing him alone, you know? Except he asked me where the cameras were. Like he missed them or something. And then, we're kissing on his couch, and he pulls away and asks me if I think he should get an agent."

D gasped. "No!"

"Yep."

"Sounds like your boy has the fame bug."

"Yeah, right? I'm hoping it's just temporary, though.

I mean, this is all pretty new for him. Maybe once the excitement wears off—"

"Hey, you two!"

Jane glanced up and saw Trevor walking toward them, coat in hand. He'd been showing up at shoots more and more lately. She hoped he hadn't overheard any of her conversation with D. "Hey, Trevor. Are you taking off?"

"Yeah, I just came by to go over a few things with Dana. Hi, D. Loved your piece about Jared Walsh."

"You didn't think I was too harsh?"

Trevor laughed. "The guy gives heterosexuality a bad name. And no, you can't quote me on that. Will we see you tonight?"

"Wouldn't miss it!"

"Great! You've done a terrific job organizing this party, Jane. Scarlett's going to be very, very happy."

"I hope so." Jane smiled, flattered. Then confused. Why did Trevor have this effect on her? When he talked to her like this, it was like he was some hard-to-please dad and she was his favorite little girl. Which was kind of weird, but it was the truth. But he could also make her feel like she was a spoiled, ungrateful brat, like when she tried to discuss the Madison Problem with him and he basically shot her down, reminding her that she got paid a lot of money to do the show. Translation: Stop being so ungrateful and suck it up.

Still . . . why did she care what he thought of her?

"She'll be here at six sharp, right, Jane?" Trevor asked.

"Um, yes. Six sharp. Dana arranged that," Jane said. She had to stop it with the psychoanalysis and focus on the party.

Trevor gave Jane a few more instructions, then said good-bye to her and D and took off. "Your boss is one good-looking man," D remarked.

Jane laughed. "D, he's, like, forty."

Jane surveyed the room to see what other area needed setting up. She noticed a small brown notebook lying on the floor nearby. She leaned over and picked it up. "This isn't yours, is it?"

D took the notebook from her and turned it over in his hand. "I wish! It's a Smythson, crocodile."

Jane's cell buzzed. She glanced at the screen and saw that it was Hannah. "D, I have to get this. See if you can figure out who it belongs to."

"No problem, sweetie."

Jane spoke briefly to Hannah, who was at OfficeMax and had a question about the poster. When she hung up, she saw that D was poring over the notebook with an intense expression. "D! I didn't tell you to snoop. I meant, look for a name or something," she teased him.

"Jane?" D looked up. "I thought your restaurant opening wasn't until next Tuesday."

Jane frowned. "It's not. Why?"

"Then why does Trevor have notes about the party from start to finish, like it's already happened?"

"Wait. That's *Trevor's* notebook?"

"Yep. He must have dropped it. Check this out." D slid the notebook across the table and stabbed his finger at an open page.

Jane stared at the entry, which was in Trevor's familiar, nearly illegible handwriting. It wasn't easy to read, but as far as Jane could tell, it said:

SIRLOIN OPENING

J arrives late, looks flustered (20–30 min late).
F's reaction = perturbed.
H already there (push her call time 30 min earlier so she's on time).
J & H discuss expectations for night while doing a task (gift bags?).
Line from J: "What could go wrong?"
M enters through side door. (Make sure to have 1 camera on J.) J won't be expecting M b/c she's not working that night. (Earlier have M say she's going to be "out of town.")
J upset that M is there.
F asks J to seat M.
Possible beat later: Chef offers girls a sample of special hors d'oeuvres (oysters, scallops?). Jane refuses (doesn't eat shellfish). Chef's reaction = insulted.

Jane gasped. WTF?

D was shaking his head. "Jane, this is just creepy. It's like you're his little puppet. He knows what you're going to do before you do."

Jane was so shocked that she could barely speak. "This . . . is . . . sick," she finally managed.

"Yeah. I mean, we all know reality TV isn't one hundred percent real, but this is crazy."

Jane began leafing through pages, growing increasingly disgusted. "Ohmigod! He's got my 'scenes' for the next three weeks all figured out. A week from Monday, I'm apparently having lunch at the Sunset Marquis with Scar, and we're apparently going to run into Madison's sister."

"Seriously?"

Jane slapped the notebook shut. She couldn't take any more of this. She picked up her cell and scrolled through her address book.

"Honey, what are you doing?" D asked her.

"Calling him. He can't treat me like this. I'm a human being!"

"No, no, *no*!" D snatched her phone away from her and tucked it into the inside pocket of his black velvet blazer. "Sweetie, you have to learn to fight fire with fire. I know you're upset, but Trevor will just talk his way out of it, and nothing's gonna change."

"But—"

"Hush! You know I'm right."

Jane fumed. D *was* right. But she couldn't just sit back

and do nothing, could she?

D squeezed her hand. "The *good* news is . . . do you understand what you have here? You have the other team's playbook."

"Huh?"

"You know exactly what Trevor has in mind for you for the next three weeks. You can be a step ahead of him the whole way. Why not use that to your advantage?"

Jane nodded slowly. D was on to something. "Yes! You're brilliant!" she said, hugging him.

"Yeah, and you thought I was just a pretty face. Come on, girl. We've got some reading to do."

22

FAME AND FORTUNE

"I'm obsessed with this," Sophie said, punching the keys on her new BlackBerry. "It's way better than my other phone. Or surfing the Web on Mom's piece-of-crap PC. It was super-sweet of Trev to give it to me. I think he really likes me, don't you?"

"Don't get too excited. We all got one. For the show," Madison explained. She looked around, wondering where in the hell the waitress was. She and Sophie were sitting at an outdoor café, waiting for the PopTV crew to show up. According to Dana's earlier email, they were going to shoot a quick scene of the two sisters discussing tonight's (*yawn*) surprise party for Scarlett.

"Check out this picture of me. Isn't it cool?" Sophie held up the screen for Madison.

Madison glanced at it. It was the same red-carpet shot from the video-game launch that had popped up all over the internet, with captions like: *L.A. CANDY*'S NEWEST

HOTTIE! and SMOKIN' SOPHIA! She fake-smiled, trying to mask her annoyance. "Yeah, it's kind of a big deal that you're my sister."

Sophie smirked. "Oh, is *that* why the photographers were all over me at the party?"

Madison rolled her eyes. "Look, everything's going really well. Let's just focus on the plan, okay?"

"What's that supposed to mean, Maddy?"

"Stop *calling* me that!"

"God, you are such a bitch today! What's the matter, did Derek stand you up again?"

"So what can I get you girls?"

The waitress had suddenly materialized at their table, pad in hand, her curious gaze bouncing between Madison and Sophie. Hopefully she hadn't overheard their conversation. "An iced soy latte, no sweetener, and make sure they actually use soy milk this time," Madison snapped.

"Got it. And for you?"

"I'll have an extra-large mocha ice-cream milk shake with whipped cream. And one of those really big chocolate-chip cookies," Sophie said, closing her menu.

"What are you, nine years old?" Madison said when the waitress had left.

"You're just mad cuz I can eat that stuff without getting fat."

Madison started to respond, then clamped her mouth shut. She wasn't going to let Sophie keep baiting her like this. "Soooo. Are you looking forward to the party?" she said in a faux-friendly voice.

"Yeah, I guess. Why are we going, though? You and that Scarlett girl hate each other, right? Or are you just pretending to hate each other for the cameras?"

"Uh, we're definitely not pretending. You and I are going because Trevor wants us there. Jane didn't invite us, so it's gonna be a big surprise. If anybody asks, we're supposed to say that Gaby invited us."

"*Did* she invite us?"

"Who knows? A PopTV assistant was handling the Evites, so Trevor probably just added our names or whatever. It doesn't matter. The point is, he wants a scene tonight when we walk into Coco de Ville, and everyone's gonna be like, 'Oh, no, what are *they* doing here?'"

"Awesome!"

Madison shrugged. "Yeah, maybe . . . if you like crashing parties where no one wants you there."

"But we're not crashing if Trev asked us to come. He's the boss," Sophie pointed out.

Madison said nothing as she watched Sophie peering around the café, adjusting her new Gucci sunglasses for what seemed like the hundredth time (the girl needed to take it easy with the "celebrity gestures") and pretending not to notice the half-dozen guys ogling her. She told herself that everything was going according to "the plan"; she had promised Sophie fame, wealth, and boyfriends in exchange for her silence, and it was already starting to happen. Sophie had been a huge hit at Playground. She'd had a ton of guys around her the entire time, and the reporters and photographers couldn't seem to get enough of her. Trevor was already talking about "maximizing Sophia's airtime."

So why did Madison feel awful? Like she'd been replaced?

She had been racking her brain trying to come up with something, *anything*, so she could regain the upper hand with Sophie. Being devious and manipulative were two of her finest qualities—normally. But the situation with Sophie was not normal, and the stress had taken a toll on Madison's creativity.

Madison Parker didn't *do* helpless. Yet that was exactly how she felt at this moment. God, how pathetic was that?

The waitress came by and set their order on the table. Sophie dug immediately into her disgusting shake and cookie. It really *was* unfair. How could she live on a diet of junk food and hard liquor and still look like *that*? Whereas Madison practically had to subsist on bottled water and carrot sticks—and spend hours a day at the gym—to maintain her size-0 body.

Sophie swiped her hand across her chocolate-stained lips. "Soooo. What's Jane's story, anyway? You guys used to be best friends, right?" she mumbled.

"That girl needs therapy. Sophie, don't talk with your mouth full."

"Who's that guy she dated? Justin?"

"Jesse. Yeah, she really screwed it up with him. I mean,

he's super-cute *and* rich. He's the son of two of the most famous actors in Hollywood, and he's a total paparazzi magnet. If he'd been *my* boyfriend, I would have done it right. You don't fall in love with a guy like that. You think with your head, not with your heart. You date him, get the press, then end it, preferably with a scandal. And you move on," Madison said.

"Yeah, makes sense," Sophie said, nodding. She seemed to be considering something. "What about Gaby? She's your friend, right?" she asked.

"Gaby's okay. She's seems to be in major makeover mode. It's probably because she got a publicist and thinks she's super-famous now."

"What's a publicist?"

"Someone who gets you into magazines and stuff."

Sophie frowned. "But . . . my picture's all over the internet. And I don't have a publicist."

"Yeah, well, a publicist can do a lot more of that."

"Do you have a publicist?"

"Not at the moment."

"Hmm, maybe I should get one, too." Sophie picked up her BlackBerry and punched some keys. "So do you just Google 'publicist,' or—"

"Sophie, it wouldn't be a good idea for you to get a publicist," Madison cut in.

"Why not?"

"It just wouldn't."

Sophie cocked her head, her eyes inscrutable behind

the dark glasses. Madison had the sudden, sinking feeling that she had just misplayed her hand. Telling Sophie not to do something almost always had the opposite effect. Like that time when they were kids and Madison told Sophie she could play with any of her dolls *except* for her special ballerina Barbie (and Madison never saw that Barbie again) . . . Anyway, Sophie was likely to go out and get herself a publicist now, which would not only triple the obnoxious amount of press coverage she was already getting (for being a new face on the show? *BFD*), but might increase both their risks of exposure, especially since Sophie seemed to have a very, very hard time keeping her damned mouth shut.

Madison glanced impatiently at her watch. Where was the PopTV van, anyway? She had to get home and get ready for the party. She really wasn't looking forward to the night ahead, but there was no escaping it . . . and besides, if she was going to play the bad-girl-slash-social-pariah (again), she might as well do it wearing her hot D&G strapless and her new black satin Loubs.

Just then, a well-dressed young guy approached their table. Madison sat up a little straighter. She knew the drill; she turned down men as a hobby.

But his eyes weren't on her . . . they were on Sophie. And Sophie was eating it up, smiling coyly and playing with her hair. Madison slid down in her chair and pretended to check her watch again. Ugh. The girl really was an attention whore.

On the other hand . . . maybe Madison was looking at this all wrong? Maybe Sophie reaping so much attention (from men, Trevor, the media) was actually a *good* thing? Up until now, Sophie held all the cards because Madison had everything to lose. But now . . . Sophie had everything to lose, too. She was starting to get a taste of fame and fortune and the perks that came with them: nice clothes, fancy cars, guys with money, VIP access. She wasn't an idiot. There was no way she was going to bring Madison down. Because if she did, she was going down, too. In flames.

Madison smiled—not a fake smile, but a *real* smile, her first one in days.

23

BIRTHDAY GIRL

Scarlett studied the contents of her closet, wondering what she should bring for her mystery overnight with Liam. She had packed jeans, shorts, T-shirts, a bathing suit, pretty lingerie, and toiletries. Just to be safe, she added a simple black tank dress, a cashmere sweater, and a pair of nice sandals. And the silver and turquoise necklace Jane had given her for her birthday last year.

She glanced at her watch. Ugh. She had to be at Coco de Ville at 6 p.m. for a "super-short pickup scene" (as Dana had described it). Scarlett would have said no, but Dana had insisted that it was a "production emergency"; apparently they had lost half the audio from the night they had filmed there (Oops! Someone just got fired.) and required a quick scene between her and Jane in order to make sense of the evening. She promised Scarlett it wouldn't take more than an hour. Scarlett had texted Liam and told him to pick her up at the club at 7 p.m. instead of at her apartment.

Scarlett wondered if Jane was already at the club. She hadn't seen her all day. She had woken up early to go to the gym, and by the time she got back, Jane was gone. It was Saturday, which was not a typical workday, although Jane often put in weekend hours, and Scarlett knew she had been busy with an upcoming restaurant opening, not to mention Aja's engagement party, which was happening in a couple of weeks.

Jane hadn't forgotten about her birthday, though. She had left a sweet note with smiley faces all over it and the message: *Happy Birthday, Scar!!!! Let's go out for birthday drinks as soon as we have a free night, okay? Love you, Jane.*

Tucker trotted into Scarlett's room and plopped down at her feet. She bent down to pet him, and he licked her face excitedly. "Aw. Thanks for my birthday kisses! Yeah, I'm turning twenty today. Isn't that crazy?"

Scarlett picked up her bag and glanced at the time on her phone: 5:35. She'd better go, or she would be late for the stupid PopTV shoot. She was dressed in the same outfit she'd worn to Coco de Ville for the original scene, so PopTV could create the illusion that this new scene wasn't being shot out of sequence. Dana had emailed her scene shots so she could match her hair, makeup, and jewelry as well. Yeah, reality.

But Scarlett didn't care. And as soon as the shoot was over . . . well, Liam would be pulling up in front of the club to pick her up. She couldn't wait to see him. She planned to throw her arms around him and kiss him for a really, really, *really* long time. . . .

"Surprrrrrrise!"

Scarlett stood inside Coco de Ville, staring dumb-founded at all the people shouting and waving and blowing noisemakers at her. A surprise party?

"Happy birthday, Scar!" Jane ran up to her and gave her a big hug. "Were you surprised? You were, weren't you?"

"Scarlett, let's get you miked right away so we can get you greeting everyone." Matt handed her a mike pack, which Scarlett automatically tucked under her blouse and clipped to the back of her skirt. At the moment, she was too numb and at a loss for words to question anything. "Oh, and happy birthday!" he added.

People began coming up to her in a flurry of hugs and kisses. "Miss Scarlett!" D screeched. "I got you the most amazing present! No, I won't give you a hint! Okay, I will. It's the most adorable little Prada bag!"

"Happy birthday, Harp. You don't look too bad for an old lady," Caleb teased her.

Naveen kissed her on the cheek. "Don't listen to him. He's just mad cuz you beat him in arm-wrestling last week."

"That's because of yours truly, her awesome personal trainer," Deb spoke up.

"This party had better be good, because I have a twenty-page paper due for linguistics on Monday," Chelsea joked.

Scarlett!

Happy birthday!

Hey, birthday girl!

Scarlett blinked, dazed and bewildered. More people came up to her and talked at her . . . a waitress handed her a glass of champagne . . . someone else put a party hat on her head . . . and all the while, flashbulbs popped in her face and the PopTV cameras zoomed in on her and Dana gestured frantically at her to do—what?

"A super-short pickup scene." Right. Scarlett couldn't believe she had fallen for Dana's dumb ruse.

Hannah from Jane's office wished her a happy birthday, as did some cute red-haired guy who had his arm around her. Peering around, Scarlett saw that the room had been decorated with balloons, streamers, and vases of yellow tulips, her favorite. A DJ was playing Kings of Leon, also her favorite. Nearby, an easel held a large collage of photos with the heading: THE SCARLETT WE KNOW AND LOVE! God, was that a picture of her sitting in a high chair, covered in spaghetti sauce? And there she was taking her first steps . . . and hugging Mickey at Disney . . . and playing Dorothy in the sixth-grade musical . . . and in braces . . . and at the prom.

I need a drink, Scarlett thought grimly, downing the glass of champagne and reaching for another, just as an elderly woman with a cane cut a path through the crowd toward her. She looked like . . .

"Grandma Harp?" Scarlett exclaimed. "I can't believe you're here!"

"I wouldn't have missed it for the world, Honey Bunny," her grandmother said warmly.

"Honey Bunny?" Deb whispered in Scarlett's ear.

"She's eighty-five," Scarlett whispered back.

"No, it's cute. I'm gonna start calling you that during our workouts."

Behind Grandma Harp were Scarlett's parents. "Hello, sweetheart," her mother said, handing her a perfectly gift-wrapped box. "It's a sweater from Saks. Tangerine. You really need to start wearing more color."

"Happy birthday, Princess," her father added. "So glad we could be here to share your big moment! Oh, and I met your new friend Naveen. We had a very nice talk about plastic surgery!"

Jane's parents and little sisters were also there. "Can I help you open your presents, Scarlett?" Nora begged.

"Yeah, and if there's anything you don't like, can I have it? Puh-lease?" Lacie added.

Jane leaned into Scarlett and whispered, "Don't worry. Family's only staying for the first hour. Then we can have a little more fun."

Gaby—or the girl who used to be Gaby, anyway—walked up to her, dragging some new faux boyfriend behind her. Scarlett had called her yesterday and tried to talk to her about her recent bizarre behavior. Gaby had replied that she had no idea what Scarlett was talking about, then ended the call, saying she was late for an appointment. Lame.

"Happy birthday, Scarlett!" Gaby said, air-kissing. "This is Roberto. He's a baseball player."

"Uh, it's hockey, actually," Roberto corrected her.

"Does *your* boyfriend know you're here with Dr. Hottie?" Gaby asked Scarlett, winking. "Don't worry, you're the birthday girl! You're allowed to hook up with anyone you want tonight!"

Scarlett gulped. *Boyfriend? Oh, no!*

"Janie!" Scarlett waved her over. "Were you in charge of this party?" she whispered.

"Yeah, Trevor asked me to organize it. I hope you don't mind!" Jane whispered back.

"It was really sweet of you. Thanks! It's just that . . . um, well, you invited Liam, right?"

"Of *course* I invited him! I mean, I didn't *personally* invite him—PopTV handled the invites." Jane looked puzzled. "But you said he was out of town this week, right? I assumed he wasn't coming."

"No. He was flying in, like, an hour ago. The thing is . . . well, never mind, I'll tell you later. I've gotta make a call."

Excusing herself, Scarlett managed to escape through the crowd and find her way to the ladies' room. It was empty. Good. She reached under her blouse and turned off the microphone (the crew would figure she wanted privacy), then pulled out her phone and dialed Liam's number. She covered her other ear with her hand, trying to drown out the loud pop music pouring over the speakers.

He answered on the first ring. "Hello?"

"Liam! Where are you?"

"Where am I? My flight was delayed. We just landed, though, so as long as the traffic cooperates, I should be at the club on time."

"You knew about the party, right?"

"Party? What are you talking about?"

"My surprise birthday party." But hearing Liam's confusion made Scarlett realize it was a surprise for him, too.

Silence. "Your . . . surprise birthday party?" Liam said finally.

"You didn't know about my party, did you?"

"No, Scarlett, I didn't know about your party."

"Jane said you were on the guest list."

"Well, my invitation must have gotten lost in the mail, then."

"Oh, God! So your birthday plans for me were real? Telling me to pack an overnight bag and stuff? You didn't just make that up so I wouldn't suspect about the party?"

"We have a dinner reservation in Malibu. And I got us a room with an ocean view at this amazing inn."

"You did?" Scarlett's heart melted. "That's so sweet!"

"Yeah, well . . . if we leave the club right at seven, we should be able to make our reservation."

"But, Liam, I can't just leave! They rented out the club for the night. Everyone's here. My eighty-five-year-old grandmother came all the way from Montecito. And the PopTV cameras are here, filming." Scarlett thought for a moment. "Why don't you come by here for a while, and we can leave for Malibu in, like, an hour or two? I don't mind eating late. I know you can't be filmed, but we can just keep you away from the cameras."

More silence.

"Liam? Are you still there?"

"You're seriously standing me up for some lame *L.A. Candy* party?"

"I am *not* standing you up! Jane organized this, and she'd be really upset if I just took off, and . . . well, besides, we can do both! I know we can! We can hang out here for a bit, then we can head up the coast and have our romantic date."

"I can't believe this," Liam said. "Your priorities are completely screwed up."

"My priorities? What are you talking about? I'm dying to see you. I haven't seen you all week! But my family and friends are all here. I can't just walk out on my own party."

"Yeah, you can. You just don't want to."

"Liam, that's not—"

"Good night, Scarlett. I hope you have a nice birthday." *Click.*

Scarlett stared at the dead phone in her hand. Had Liam just hung up on her? What the hell? How could he not understand the predicament she was in? Maybe she hadn't explained things clearly enough. . . .

She started to redial his number when Dana rushed into the ladies' room. "Scarlett! There you are! We need you out here right this second!" she said.

"What? Why?"

"Cuz they're about to bring out your cake. Come on, come on!"

"Fine! I'm coming!"

Sighing, Scarlett tucked her phone back in her pocket and switched her mike back on. As she followed Dana out of the ladies' room, she caught sight of her own reflection in the mirror. Her face looked tense and unhappy. She hated fighting with Liam. An hour ago, she had been packing her bag, wondering what amazing surprise he had in store for her birthday.

Malibu. A little inn by the sea. It was just like Liam to dream up something like that.

And now, she was stuck at this party . . . and he was mad at her. How had everything gotten so twisted around?

Walking out of the ladies' room, Scarlett saw the crowd—*her* crowd—having fun, drinking champagne, dancing to the Black Eyed Peas. She took a deep breath and plastered a big smile on her face. It was time to play the birthday girl, at least for a little while longer, until she could slip away and go find Liam and make up. If it wasn't too late.

Then Jane rushed to her side, her face as tense and

unhappy as Scarlett's had been in the ladies' room mirror before. "Hey. What's up?" Scarlett asked her curiously.

Jane nodded toward the doorway. "Guess what just walked in?"

Scarlett followed Jane's gaze. Madison and Sophia were standing there, wearing variations on the same strapless metallic Spandex dress, smiling and waving as though they were on the red carpet. Gaby was walking up to them, air-kissing and clinging to her hockey-player "boyfriend."

"I'm assuming you didn't invite them," Scarlett whispered to Jane.

"Uh, no. Gaby told me *she* invited them. But honestly? I think Trevor messed with the guest list when the Evites were getting sent out."

Yeah, Trevor messed with the guest list all right, Scarlett thought, thinking of Liam. It all made sense now. Trevor would not have wanted Liam at the party—not just because Liam couldn't be filmed, but because it would interfere with whatever trumped-up "flirtation" scenes Trevor had in mind for Scarlett and Naveen.

Could this birthday get any worse?

24

TWO STEPS AHEAD

It was just before 5 p.m. on Tuesday when Jane strolled into Sirloin, feeling very put together in a navy skirt and crisp white blouse and with her hair styled in a neat ponytail. Good. Her appearance as she made her grand entrance would be the opposite of "flustered," which is what Trevor was expecting from her, and at 5:30, no less.

"Hi, Dana!" Jane breezed past the producer and went up to one of the sound guys. "Hey, Jack. I'm ready to be miked. I like your T-shirt!"

"Thanks!" Jack grinned and handed her a pack.

"Jane?" Dana looked totally confused. "We . . . uh . . . we weren't . . . ."

"I know I'm a little early, but I wanted to make sure everything was running smoothly," Jane said, smiling innocently.

The door opened, and Hannah walked into the restaurant. Her cheeks were flushed as though she'd been rushing. "Hi, Dana, hi, Jack! Jane, you beat me here! Wow, that's gotta be a first, right?" she joked.

"Ha-ha. Is Fiona here?" Jane asked Dana.

"Uh . . . not yet. She should be here any sec. Uh, why don't you girls get miked, then we can get a quick scene with you stuffing gift bags?"

"That sounds great!" Jane said eagerly, as though stuffing gift bags was the most thrilling activity, ever.

Dana, Hannah, and Jack all stared at her.

"So *you're* in a cheerful mood," Hannah said to Jane as they tucked gift certificates, wine stoppers, and bottles of gourmet steak sauce into small black-and-white totes with the Sirloin logo.

"Yeah, it's been a good day. I went to the gym, then I had lunch with Aja's publicist, Wanda, to discuss the Vegas party, then I spent the afternoon doing errands for tonight."

"I think it's just you and me on duty this evening. Oliver's studying for finals, and I guess Madison's out of town?"

"Apparently." Jane pretended to search for a missing wine stopper as she tried to keep a straight face. She had to act as though she had no idea she was about to get "ambushed" by Madison, who wasn't out of town at all. "Soooo. You and Oliver looked pretty cozy at Scarlett's birthday party."

Hannah blushed. "Yeah, he's really sweet. And he

loves the same things I do!"

"Like?"

"Like . . . old movies. And cooking. And hiking in Joshua Tree. *And* my parents like him."

"He's met your parents? That's huge!"

"It was totally low-key. They took us out to dinner last week. My dad's kind of overprotective and asked Oliver about a billion questions. Oliver was cool about it." She added, "We're going to San Diego so I can meet his parents, maybe next weekend."

"Wow."

Hannah smiled dreamily and stared off into space as she finished up a gift bag. Jane watched her and thought about Caleb. She didn't feel about him the way Hannah seemed to feel about Oliver. (Or how Scar felt about Liam . . . although Liam had never made it to the birthday party on Saturday, and now the two of them seemed to be fighting, although Jane wasn't positive because Scar didn't want to talk about it.) But maybe it was a good thing Jane wasn't head over heels about Caleb, since they were hanging out and not heading down the aisle. Okay, so she missed the heady wanting-to-make-out-all-the-time chemistry (the way it used to be for them in high school). But she didn't miss the Jesse-style insanity.

And she really wasn't into Caleb's slightly-too-keen interest in being filmed. And photographed by the paparazzi. And in general being a "celebrity." Jane hoped it was a phase, one that he would outgrow soon. She remembered, he went through a similar phase senior year, when the swim team won the national championship. Being team captain, he was interviewed for a dozen newspaper articles and even appeared on a couple of local news channels. The attention had gone to his head for a while. It had been annoying until he finally got over it and returned to his old self.

Her cell buzzed. It was a text from Dana:

PLZ DISCUSS OPENING TONITE, EVERYTHINGS GOING WELL, ETC. FINISH WITH LINE: WHAT COULD GO WRONG?

Jane smiled serenely at Dana, who was watching her from across the room along with Trevor and Fiona, and tucked her phone back into her pocket. It was pretty awesome, being two steps ahead of the higher-ups, for a change. "So. I'm seating the guests tonight. Can you manage the press line?" she asked Hannah.

"No problem." Hannah peered at her watch. "People are going to start to arrive soon. I should check in with the chef to make sure the passed hors d'oeuvres are ready to go."

"Great! Hey, I meant to tell you . . . I love the flowers you picked out. And the menu cards are really cool, too."

"Thanks!"

Jane glanced around the 1940s-style dining room with its wine-colored leather booths, black and white tiles, silver wall sconces, and framed photos of movie stars. There were votives and flowers on every table, along with place settings and ivory cards engraved with tonight's special menu. The place looked beautiful and elegant, all ready for its grand opening.

"Everything's going so well," Jane recited, as if from a teleprompter. "What could go wrong?"

Hannah gave her a funny look. "Um, nothing? This night's gonna be perfect! Don't jinx it, Jane!"

Jane grinned. "I won't."

"Hi, Ashley, hi, Scott, it's so nice to see you both! Follow me . . . right this way."

Jane led Ashley Pierce and her fiancé to their seats in the center of the room. It was an art, planning the seating chart for an event, especially when there were celebrities involved. Celebrities meant fragile (actually, more like combustible) egos as well as constantly shifting friendships, relationships, alliances. Jane couldn't seat Ashley at the same table as Leda Phillips, since the two had competed for the same role in an upcoming film. (Leda won.) And Jared Walsh couldn't be anywhere near Aidan Kline, since Jared had not-so-secretly hooked up with Aidan's then-girlfriend last year at Cannes. Joe Giardi, one of the most powerful agents in Hollywood, had to have the best table in the house—or should she give it to Carly Henek, who had recently and very publicly cut ties with the A-list rep?

As soon as Jane had seated Ashley and her fiancé, she

headed back toward the end of the press line, where more celebrities would be waiting for their tables. On the way, she noticed two PopTV camera guys parked by a side entrance . . . and a third PopTV camera guy nearby, his camera focused on Jane.

This was it. Jane was ready. She stopped in her tracks and pretended to adjust her earpiece. Just then, the door opened, and Madison sauntered in.

Out of the corner of her eye, Jane saw that the first camera was trained on Madison (who was already miked—Jane could just make out the faint outline of a pack under her dress), and the second camera was trained on Jane. The third camera was trained on Fiona, who was hurrying through the dining room toward the two girls.

Madison tossed her hair over her shoulders and smiled smugly at Jane.

"Jane, could you—" Fiona began.

"Hey, Madison! So nice to see you!" Jane said in an extra-friendly voice. "I knew you might be out of town, but I saved you a table just in case. Follow me!"

Madison's smile disappeared from her face. Fiona looked stunned.

Jane had to resist the urge to laugh. This was too awesome. She couldn't wait to see what would happen next.

"Hey, can you seat us at Madison's table, too?"

Jane turned around at the sound of the familiar voice. It couldn't be . . .

It *was.*

Jesse was standing there, looking impossibly handsome in a black tailored shirt and slacks. On his arm was Sophia Parker.

Madison seemed just as surprised as Jane. "Sophia, are you *serious*?" she hissed.

Sophia smirked. "I need a drink. You need a drink, sweetie?" she said, caressing Jesse's arm.

Jesse kissed Sophia on the lips. "Oh, yeah. Where's the bar in this place?"

Jane was completely speechless. This was definitely not in the book.

25

JUST US GIRLS

"Can you pass the ketchup?" Gaby asked Madison as she reached for another french fry. "Annabelle wouldn't let me eat in front of the press, so I'm starving! I mean, what kind of publicist doesn't let you eat steak at the grand opening of a restaurant called Sirloin?"

"Yeah, that sucks," Madison agreed, handing her the ketchup bottle. The two girls were sitting in Mel's Drive-In, which was almost empty at this late hour on a Tuesday night (or was it Wednesday morning now?).

Madison rubbed her temples, which were beginning to throb from one too many martinis at the opening and from the shock of seeing Sophie and Jesse Edwards together. "How's Annabelle working out for you, anyway? She seems to be getting you a lot of press," she said, trying to make conversation.

"Yeah, she's really good!" Gaby agreed. "Except . . ."

"Except what?"

"Except . . . she makes me do all this stuff. Like, I have to get my hair and makeup done before every single shoot. And she has me working with this stylist who totally changed the way I dress. At first it was kinda fun, but now I don't feel like me. I feel like I'm playing a part." Gaby tugged at her tight black minidress, which made her new cleavage bunch up and practically spill out. "Plus . . . my boobs *hurt*."

"Yeah, I heard breast surgery can be like that," Madison said, not revealing the fact that she'd had the procedure done herself, more than once. "But this is Hollywood. If you don't keep up with all the other skinny, gorgeous double-D girls, you're out."

"Yeah. But I'm also sick of the stuff Annabelle's making me say on the show and in the magazines. She and Trevor have these meetings, and then she tells me that I have to be a bitch to Jane and Scarlett if I want more airtime. I know, I know!" she added quickly when Madison shot her an annoyed look. "You hate their guts. But I'm kinda friends with them *and* with you. I'm sorry, but I'm just being honest. I don't like taking sides or being mean to anybody. Besides, I thought the whole point of being on a reality show is that you get to be yourself. Well, this isn't me."

Madison took a sip of her sparkling water. Unlike Gaby, she was not going to let her bad mood push her to eat french fries and fatty little sliders. So. Gaby's sleazy new publicist was behind her new look and personality.

And it was obviously paying off. Madison had noticed a lot more of Gaby in the magazines and on Season 2 of the show.

Part of her was tempted to tell Gaby to stop whining. She had what she wanted, didn't she? More fame, more airtime, more boyfriends? (Even though the "boyfriends" were just in it for the media attention.)

Gaby also didn't have half the problems Madison had. Not nearly. Madison was still reeling from the idea of Sophie hooking up with Jesse. No wonder the little bitch was grilling her on Saturday about him and the other people on *L.A. Candy*. She had obviously been searching for a way to make a big tabloid splash. Showing up at the restaurant opening with Jane's fresh-out-of-rehab ex definitely qualified. As for Jesse, what better way for him to get back at Jane for dumping him than dating her cute new costar (and Madison's sister, although frankly, dating Madison herself would have meant *way* higher ratings)? Jane (who had seemed strangely giddy about spending her evening stuffing gift bags and seating celebs) had not been able to mask her shock at seeing the happy new couple. And she had not been able to hide her disgust as she watched them downing vodka shot after vodka shot and showing way too much PDA in front of the A-list crowd.

Madison had wondered briefly if Trevor had arranged for Sophie and Jesse to show up at the party together, for the publicity or just for "drama" on the show. But from the stunned expression on Trevor's face at their grand entrance, it had been just as much of a surprise for him as everyone else.

Sophie was clearly after the spotlight—and she was succeeding, so far. Which meant that Madison had both Sophie *and* Jane to worry about now. Because there was only room in the spotlight for one of them. Sophie was allowed to be famous, sure—but not more famous than Madison. Not anywhere close.

Gaby's voice interrupted her worries. "It's been so long, just us girls hanging out without the cameras. I mean, it's hard to imagine now, but there once was a time when we all kinda got along. Hey, I know! You wanna come with me when I walk Princess Baby?" she said eagerly.

"That sounds great, but I'm really tired, and I've gotta be at the office early," Madison fibbed. Of course, she had no intention of showing up at Fiona's in the morning or any time tomorrow, for that matter.

Besides, she was curious to see if Sophie was home— and if so, if she was alone. After tonight, Madison realized that she was going to have to be more vigilant than ever about her baby sister. Sophie was beating Madison at her own game.

26

RELATIONSHIP PROBLEMS

Scarlett tried to pay attention to what Professor Friedman was saying about their latest assignment, *Manon Lescaut* by Antoine François Prévost. She had just started reading the eighteenth-century French novel about a nobleman and his girlfriend who had serious relationship problems.

Yeah, join the club, Scarlett thought with a heavy sigh.

She and Liam had not spoken since her birthday party four days ago. He had texted her later that night, saying that he needed to "take a break," whatever that meant. In response, she had started about twenty different emails to him, but ended up hitting Delete each time, because she couldn't seem to express exactly what she was feeling.

Which was that she missed him. And that she was mad at him. And that she was mad at herself.

She was mad at Liam because he wouldn't meet her halfway that night and just make an *appearance* at Coco de Ville. Of course she knew he couldn't be filmed. She got that. But he could have avoided the cameras and hung out with their friends at an out-of-the-way table until it was cool for the two of them to slip away . . . at which point they could have driven to that romantic little inn in Malibu and *really* celebrated her birthday.

She was also mad at herself because she couldn't seem to figure out how to meet *him* halfway. Not just about her birthday, but generally speaking. She knew that dating her was making it hard for him to get work. Since *Gossip* magazine outed them as a couple (and PopTV fired him as a result), producers weren't sure they could trust him not to try to date the "talent" on their own shows. She also knew how much he hated watching the recent *L.A. Candy* episode where Trevor had somehow managed to make her scenes with Naveen look seriously flirtatious. In one case, he had patched together a shot of Scarlett staring intently at (probably) the wall . . . and a shot of Naveen staring intently at (probably) a hot waitress . . . and set the whole thing to "You and Me" by Lifehouse, resulting in a cliff-hanger brimming with romantic tension. Gross.

Of course, Liam, being a former PopTV employee, was well aware of Trevor's creative use of editing techniques and cheesy soundtracks. But still, it couldn't be easy for him.

Which left the ball in Scarlett's court. Could she stand up to Trevor and demand that he stop using her so shame-lessly for ratings? She had promised him that she would be more cooperative this season and not take everything so seriously. So far, she'd been successful—hadn't she? Unfortunately, her "success" had taken its toll on her relationship with Liam. She wasn't sure how much more he was going to put up with. And now there was Liam's Evite mysteriously disappearing into the void.

To make things even worse . . . the day after the birthday party, Jane had shown her a little brown notebook belonging to Trevor. She'd found it at Coco de Ville during the setup for the party. Most of the pages were filled with gibberish—Trevor's handwriting was even worse than Jane's—but Scarlett had been able to make out enough of it, with Jane's help, to see how obsessed he was with plotting the girls' "scenes" on the show. It was as though he were writing a script from scratch, not producing a reality show.

Scarlett hadn't been surprised to learn that Trevor's mind worked this way. But she *had* been surprised (and shocked and disturbed) by how much he'd lied to her and the others to get them to do his bidding.

So basically, she had been wrong about what she told Liam over dinner last week: She *was* Trevor's puppet, which was the last thing she wanted to be. Between that and Liam's unhappiness with the show . . . Well, one option would be to bail after Season 2. Sure, the money was great, and she loved being financially independent from her parents. But there had to be other gigs out there that paid well and didn't require her to feel so manipulated and that would allow her to be with a guy who didn't want to be on TV.

Or maybe she should quit the show but postpone the job hunting. Maybe she should just suck it up and let her parents support her until she graduated from college and started her *real* career, whatever that was. (She'd had some fantasies recently about becoming a journalist—not a faux journalist, like the tabloid idiots who wanted to know what her favorite ice-cream flavor was, but a real journalist.) The question was . . . which college? She'd gotten five more acceptances since Columbia, and she was still waiting to hear from a few others. Pretty soon, she was going to have to make a decision: to transfer or not to transfer? And she was going to have to tell Liam, either way. (And Jane.)

If she transferred, she would have to leave Jane . . . and possibly leave Liam, unless he decided to relocate with her. That could be cool, being in a new city with Liam. But what if he didn't *want* to relocate—or *couldn't* because he was on the brink of his dream job right here in L.A.? If their roles were reversed, would she do the same for him? If he told her tomorrow that he had received an amazing opportunity that meant moving far away, would she follow him?

This was all assuming they still had a relationship to negotiate over. Which was questionable, since they weren't even speaking.

She groaned and dropped her face into her hands, wondering how her life had gotten so complicated.

An IM popped up on her laptop screen. WAKE UP! Chelsea had written.

Scarlett glanced across the room. Chelsea gave her a little wave. Up front, Professor Friedman was scribbling on the chalkboard and talking about the poor nobleman trying to please his girlfriend, who had expensive tastes.

Hmm, sounds like a perfect reality show, Scarlett thought wryly. She typed, I AM AWAKE. IM JUST TRYING TO FIGURE OUT MY LIFE.

I CAN HELP WITH THAT. DRINK LATER? Chelsea replied.

YES, PLEASE! Scarlett typed.

WELL IF I MANAGE TO FIGURE OUT YOUR LIFE, DRINKS ARE ON YOU :-)

Scarlett smiled to herself. If Chelsea could solve all her problems, she would be happy to buy her whatever the hell she wanted.

27

THAT CRAZY, LOVESICK GIRL

"I'm sorry I couldn't make your restaurant opening. How'd it go?" Caleb asked Jane. He reached across the table and lightly stroked her arm.

She smiled and squeezed his hand before reaching into her purse for her lip gloss and compact, trying to buy herself an extra moment to formulate a response. Because how should she answer this question? *It was awesome! My crazy ex-boyfriend, who just got out of rehab, showed up at the party with Madison's little sister. I think they went through most of the vodka in the place. And I'm afraid to leave my apartment because there are paps with camcorders camped outside, wanting a quote from me about the two of them hooking up. A couple of mornings, I had to have one of the PopTV production vans pick me up at the side gate so I could avoid them. . . .*

Of course, she couldn't say any of that, since the PopTV cameras were filming their dinner date at Katsuya. Instead she replied, "It was fine. Now I'm totally focused on Aja's

227

party next weekend. There's still so much to do!"

"I am definitely *not* missing that one," Caleb said, taking a sip of his drink. "I've never been to Vegas. It's pretty wild there, right?"

"It's a lot of fun."

"What happens in Vegas stays in Vegas?" Caleb joked.

"That's what they say." Jane forced a laugh. "Hey, here's our food."

The waitress set their appetizers on the table: a green salad for Jane and raw oysters for Caleb. Jane used to come to Katsuya a lot with Jesse; it was one of his favorite restaurants in L.A., although probably not anymore, not since their disastrous date in January when she'd confessed to having met up with Braden earlier that day. Jesse hadn't taken it too well. . . .

Jane had tried to avoid Jesse at Sirloin the other night; she hadn't been up to a confrontation or even a conversation, under the circumstances. But he had managed to corner her briefly while Sophia was in the ladies' room.

"Well, look at you, Jane. Working hard at your important job?" he had said in a gruff, slurry voice, his hot breath reeking of alcohol. "Yeah, you definitely didn't waste any time getting a new boyfriend. Not that I give a damn. I'm hooking up with Sophia now. I guess you can say I upgraded."

Jane—aware that there were at least two cameras trained on her—had simply replied that she was happy to see that his rehab had paid off, then excused herself. It was a low blow, but it would also make it difficult for Trevor to use the scene, since he would never address Jesse's alcoholism on the show. Although knowing Trevor, he would probably find a way.

"You want one of these? They're pretty tasty," Caleb said, offering her an oyster.

"Um, no, thanks," Jane said, making a face. She didn't know how he could eat those slimy things. Gross.

Jane's cell buzzed. She sighed. *Of course* it was a text from Dana:

YOU'RE ON A DATE WITH YOUR BF. SMILE!

Jane groaned inwardly as she placed her cell back in her lap, took a deep breath, and forced a smile. She knew all about Trevor's efforts to try to "heat up" her and Caleb's relationship from reading his little notebook. Was their chemistry, or rather, lack of chemistry, *that* obvious? That was kind of sad. But watching the last few episodes of the show, Jane *had* noticed that she and Caleb weren't the most exciting couple ever. Of course he was gorgeous (he already had a huge female fan base from the show), and of course they had fun together. But something was . . . *missing.* And things had become kind of strained between them lately because of his continued obsession with being filmed, photographed, and interviewed. She was starting to wonder if he actually *liked* her, or if he was just with her for the media attention. What had he said to her at STK?

229

You know me, Janie. I'm your biggest fan, and I'll always be your biggest fan. Not because you're a star, but because you're Janie Roberts from Santa Barbara who saves stray animals and likes to eat Cheerios out of an Elmo bowl.

What happened to that Caleb?

As for Trevor's notebook . . . well, it was a gold mine, but it was a curse, too. Jane spent way too much time going through it and plotting ways to mess with Trevor's head. She'd wasted her entire lunch hour yesterday figuring out how to foil his plans for her in the coming weeks. She was going to "run into" Madison at Kate Somerville on Tuesday? She would tell her how pretty her manicure was! She and Caleb were going to "run into" Jesse and Sophia at Beso on Thursday night? She would tell Sophia that she should order the Bibb salad!

But frankly . . . Jane wasn't sure she would follow through with either idea. The game was already growing tiresome, and eventually, she would have to face the *real* problem, which was that Trevor treated her like she was a mouse in a maze—*his* mouse in *his* maze that he had carefully constructed with a predetermined outcome.

Jane was still trying to make out some of the entries—Trevor's handwriting was a disaster—and trying to understand some of them, too. There were entries about Scar and Naveen (which Scar was not happy about when Jane had shown her) and also Madison, Gaby, Hannah, and Sophia. But there was one entry which Jane couldn't figure out at all. It seemed to be about a guy, and the entry had

230

intrigued her because the guy in question didn't appear to be either Caleb or Naveen. She reminded herself to make another stab at deciphering that entry later.

Her cell buzzed again. *Oh, God, Dana.* Without bothering to read the text, Jane automatically reached across the table and laced her fingers through Caleb's. "This place is nice, isn't it?" was all she could manage to come up with. She was out with her handsome boyfriend on a Saturday night, having dinner at a trendy L.A. restaurant. So why wasn't she enjoying herself?

"Yeah, it's pretty cool. Hey, what are you doing tomorrow? Dodgers have a home game, and Naveen and I were thinking of going. Maybe you and Scar could come with us?"

"Love to, but I've gotta go into the office," Jane said apologetically. "I know, I know, it's a Sunday . . . but I'm meeting with Hannah to go over some stuff for Vegas."

Jane's cell buzzed almost immediately. She already knew what it was going to say:

JANE, WHAT MEETING WITH HANNAH? SHE'S OUT OF TOWN. SAY YES!!!!!!

Jane knew Hannah was in San Diego, visiting with Oliver's parents. She felt bad lying to Caleb. But she'd had a lot of Caleb time lately. She could use a day off.

Caleb grinned. "I wish Principal Enemark could see you now. If you'd worked half this hard in high school, you would've gotten straight As instead of—"

"Okay, that's enough," Jane cut in, laughing.

The rest of the evening was fine, mostly talking about whether or not Caleb would return to Yale in the fall. He seemed as though he was leaning toward it, in part because his parents were putting pressure on him to finish his education . . . and much to Jane's surprise, she didn't feel bothered by it. But shouldn't she feel *something*? When he left for Yale the first time, to start his freshman year, she had missed him so much, so achingly. They had called and texted several times a day (at least for a while, until he stopped being quite so attentive). She had put photos of him on all her screensavers and never taken off the silver heart necklace he had given her for graduation.

So what happened to that crazy, lovesick girl?

Jane's cell rang as she drove down Hollywood Boulevard. She and Caleb had decided to spend the night at their own apartments since Jane had to "work" in the morning.

She glanced at her phone, figuring it would be Dana or maybe yet another reporter wanting a quote about Jesse and Sophia . . . and was surprised to see BRADEN CALLING pop up.

She felt breathless. She hadn't spoken to him since he left for Banff a month ago. She tapped on her Bluetooth. "Hello?"

"Hey." Braden sounded relieved that she had picked up. "Is this a bad time?"

"No, not at all! How *are* you?" Jane couldn't believe he was calling. She also couldn't believe how happy it made her.

"Good. Tired. We've been shooting, like, twelve hours a day every day. A lot of the scenes are outdoors, in the snow and wind."

"Sounds intense."

"Yeah, it is, but it's going really well. My part's awesome. I can't wait to take you to see the final cut."

"Yeah, I can't wait, either."

"So . . . how's my favorite reality-TV star? Any good gossip?"

Jane giggled. "Oh, yes. I have so much to tell you!"

"Yeah? A couple of the girls I'm shooting with love your show. They're obsessed with that Caleb guy. I didn't even know you had a boyfriend again."

Jane was speechless for a second. She hadn't expected this. "He's a good friend," she said defensively. Which wasn't exactly the truth. Why was she acting like this, like she was cheating on Braden with Caleb and had to lie to Braden about it? She and Braden weren't together—far from it.

"Oh."

Silence.

"So what are you up to tonight?" Jane said, hoping to change the subject.

"Uh . . . well, I'm going to a bar called the Hibernating Bear to meet some people."

"Sounds fun."

"Yeah. You'd like it; it's really low-key, and they make the best burgers."

"Is it better than Big Wangs?"

"Wow. Big Wangs is a hard one to beat. Especially since that's where you and I met."

Jane blinked. This was the closest Braden had ever come to saying something heartfelt to her.

Braden coughed a little. "Anyway . . . I think the film's gonna be wrapping in the next couple of weeks. We're actually ahead of schedule."

"That's awesome!"

"Maybe we can hang out when I get back?"

"Sure. Can't wait," Jane said, meaning it.

They continued talking as Jane drove home, parked her car, and went up to her apartment, where she ran into Scar watching TV in the living room, alone (on a Saturday night—where was Liam?). By the time she and Braden said their good-byes, well after midnight, she realized that she was finally feeling what she should have been feeling with Caleb earlier.

Only she wasn't feeling it for Caleb.

This is so mixed up, Jane told herself.

28

THE CENTERPIECE OF *L.A. CANDY*

It was late Sunday night, and Trevor was alone in his office at PopTV. He hit the Rewind button on the remote and watched carefully as the latest cut of this week's episode replayed on his wall-mounted flat-screen. There was Jane arriving early at Sirloin, despite the fact that Dana had specifically told her to be there a half hour later. He hit Fast Forward. There was Jane, cheerfully seating Madison before Fiona instructed her to do so. He hit Fast Forward again, to another scene in which Jane, Madison, and Hannah were having a meeting about Aja's party. Jane was *supposed* to be shocked and upset when Madison announced that she had called the people at the Venetian and completely changed the menu. But Jane had reacted with perfect calm, thanking Madison for her help and adding that she had *just* spoken to the head chef herself and changed everything back.

What . . . the . . . hell?

Trevor leaned back in his leather chair and steepled his hands under his chin. There was only one explanation. Jane was on to him. He had misplaced his Smythson notebook about a week ago, maybe at Coco de Ville. Obviously, Jane had found it, or someone else had found it and was leaking the information to her.

And now Jane was going rogue on him, doing and saying whatever she damned well pleased on camera. She was even being nice to Madison, which was completely inconsistent with their enormously popular feud. Frenemies were good for ratings; polite work colleagues were most definitely not.

This had to stop. The question was, how? He could try the direct approach: calling Jane into his office, saying he knew about the notebook, and telling her point-blank that she had to start being more cooperative, or else. She was, undeniably, one of America's most popular young celebrities. Did she really want to lose all that now?

Trevor sighed and reached for his glass of scotch; he always had a drink, just one, after he was done editing for the night.

It didn't help, either, that Jane's "romance" with Caleb was such a disappointment. Frankly, it would be better for ratings if she got back together with Jesse Edwards. Not that that could or should happen, but still. Trevor would have to use every trick in the book while editing Jane's last few dates with Caleb, just to keep viewers from falling asleep in their chairs.

At least the rest of the show was going well. Scarlett wasn't giving him a hard time this season, thank God, and the new Gaby was a hit, thanks to her shamelessly aggressive publicist. The Hannah-Oliver story line was also pulling respectable interest. Trevor had chosen well with Oliver, who was playing his part beautifully.

And Sophia. Sophia was a gold mine. Not only was she gorgeous, but she seemed desperate for attention and willing to do whatever it took to get it, which were excellent qualities for a reality show. Trevor had been thrilled when she showed up at Sirloin unexpectedly with Jesse (although he had cringed moments later when they started hitting the booze like a couple of out-of-control drunks). Still, maybe there was a way to let Sophia be Sophia while reining her in just enough to make sure she didn't do something completely crazy. Trevor would have to think of some story lines for her that would maximize her potential and increase her airtime.

Which would probably not make Madison too happy. What was it between those two, anyway? If she didn't want her sister on the show, why had she hand-delivered her to him? Trevor could practically feel Madison's blood pressure rising every time Sophia entered the room. Hmmm, maybe that could be one of Sophia's story lines: a sister-sister feud. That might divert attention from the nonevent Jane and Madison's feud had become lately.

Trevor took another sip of scotch. Back to Jane. He had to solve that problem, fast. No matter what, she was the centerpiece of *L.A. Candy*. Madison, Sophia, Gaby, even Scarlett and Hannah—they were all *characters*. Jane was *real*. He couldn't let her slip away from him. And he couldn't let her reality continue to descend into *ordinary*.

He hit the Fast Forward button again, to Jane's dinner date last night with Caleb.

Caleb. Trevor leaned forward, an interesting new idea forming in his head. Maybe the boring boyfriend was part of the solution?

29

ABSOLUTELY, POSITIVELY, MADLY

"If I was single, I would so be throwing myself at that guy right this second," Scarlett remarked. "Oh . . . my . . . God."

Jane grinned. "Yeah. You and every other girl here. Aja might have something to say about that, though."

In a large reception room at the Venetian, Aja and Miguel were getting ready for their much-anticipated engagement-party-slash-masked-ball. An entourage of harried-looking stylists, assistants, and others were doing a last-minute check of the couple's outfits (a black tux for him, a long black-and-white evening gown for her, and jewel-studded black masks for both), while a line of photographers stood by, ready to snap away, and several bodyguards secured the area. There were PopTV crew, hotel employees, and others floating around the room as well.

Scarlett was hanging out with Jane, just killing time until Dana or whoever came by and rounded them up for filming. (Aja had graciously consented to PopTV inviting Scarlett, Gaby, Sophia, and a few other *L.A. Candy* cast members and their friends to the party, so they could make an episode out of it.) Every once in a while, Jane would make a random comment about the guest list or the bar, which had confused Scarlett at first, until she realized that Jane was communicating with Hannah on her earpiece.

"Speaking of *not* being single . . . where's your boyfriend?" Jane asked Scarlett.

"What? Oh. He, uh, couldn't make it," Scarlett said.

Jane gave her a pointed look. "Scar, what is going on with you two?"

Scarlett fidgeted with her gold cuff bracelet, which she was supposed to tell reporters was a Mandy Monk original, and tried to figure out how to answer that question. She and Liam had continued with their "break" these last couple of weeks, with no phone calls or texts or emails whatsoever. And she had been deeply miserable the entire time. Before Liam, she used to think that she could happily stay single forever. Not anymore. Forget Aja's hot fiancé— or any other guy, for that matter. She wanted only Liam. She just wasn't sure if Liam still wanted *her*.

Scarlett peered around the room, stalling, hoping Jane would just drop the subject, already—and noticed Gaby and her publicist in the corner having a heated conversation. A beat later, Gaby glanced in Scarlett and Jane's direction and shook her head, obviously upset. What was going on?

Before Scarlett could mention what she saw to Jane, she felt Jane squeeze her hand. "You know you can tell me if something's wrong."

"What? Yeah, I know. Thanks, Janie."

"Is everything okay with you and Liam?"

Scarlett sighed. "No. We're *not* okay," she blurted out. "I think he's ready to break up with me over this stupid show."

"Oh, no! Because of Naveen?"

"That, and . . . I'm always shooting, and Liam can't be filmed, so we don't have a lot of time to be together. Plus, it's been hard for him to find another job because of me. Oh, and the night of my birthday party . . . well, I think Trevor or somebody 'lost' his Evite, and Liam had these big surprise plans to take me to Malibu. He had the whole evening planned."

Jane gasped. "Are you serious? Trevor told me he was going to talk to Liam about the party and clear it with him."

"Well, obviously, Trevor 'forgot.' Or, more likely, he lied to you. Anyway, that's not your fault, and besides, my party was amazing. Thank you for organizing it." Scarlett paused, searching for the right words. "The truth is . . . I need to figure some stuff out. Like what's important to me."

"Yeah. You need to choose between the show and the guy you care about," Jane said.

And college, Scarlett added silently. On the plane ride

to Las Vegas, she had finally made her decision. She was going to transfer out of USC in the fall. Which was going to mean leaving L.A.

"Listen, there's something else——" Scarlett began.

"Jane! Scarlett! I've been looking all over for you girls!"

Scarlett saw Dana marching toward them, a walkie-talkie in one hand and a clipboard in the other. "You two have to get miked *now*! Jane, we need to shoot a super-quick scene of you and Hannah doing some final prep. And, Scarlett, you need to get over to St. Mark's Square ASAP."

Jane looked alarmed. "Final prep? What final prep? Everything's all set."

"Just make up some minor crisis. It doesn't matter. We need a couple of mike packs over here, please!" Dana shouted to one of the sound guys.

Jane squeezed Scarlett's hand again. "To be continued," she whispered, out of Dana's earshot. "About Liam . . . don't worry. You guys are in love, and you belong together. It's gonna be okay."

"Yeah, I hope so."

Scarlett gave Jane a quick hug. In love? They had never said, "I love you." But Scarlett knew it was true. It's too bad that it almost took breaking up for her to realize it.

Scarlett finished getting miked and headed for the doorway. She noticed that Gaby and her publicist were gone—in fact, everyone seemed to be spilling out of the room and into the hallway. Jane had mentioned that Aja and

Miguel were going to be boarding a gondola somewhere soon, then traveling via canal to the St. Mark's Square part of the hotel. There, they would make their grand entrance in front of hundreds of masked guests. Soooo Vegas!

Then Scarlett caught sight of Aja and Miguel at the back of the pack, momentarily alone. The couple exchanged a quick, tender kiss before rejoining their entourage.

God, they're actually in love, Scarlett thought, surprised. *It's not just for the cameras or for publicity.*

Scarlett pulled her cell out of her clutch to check the time. If she hurried now, maybe she could make a late flight back to L.A.? She could pack her bag, leave a quick note for Dana along with her mike pack (*Sorry, family emergency!*), and send Jane a text (IT'S ALL GOOD. LUV U). And then she could rush home and find Liam and tell him what she should have told him a long time ago.

Which was that she was absolutely, positively, madly in love with him. He was pretty much the best thing that had happened to her, ever.

She was also going to tell him about her decision to leave the show and USC and transfer to a new college. How would he take the news? Would he scoop her up in his arms and vow to follow her to Yale or Harvard or wherever because he was in love with her, too, and he couldn't live without her? *(Yeah, wishful thinking.)*

Flush with nervousness and excitement, Scarlett turned on her way-too-high designer heels and half ran, half hobbled to the elevator banks. She felt strangely free.

Once on the ninth floor, she rushed out of the elevator—and stopped in her tracks. A PopTV camera guy and Matt the director were positioned a little ways down the hall. They had their backs to her, and the camera guy was filming a girl with big hair and a ruffly red dress walking into one of the rooms.

Scarlett frowned. Wait, was that *her* room?

After a moment, Scarlett realized that no, that *wasn't* her room, which was two doors to the left of the elevators; it was actually Jane and Caleb's room, which was two doors to the *right*. She also remembered that Gaby was wearing a dress just like that downstairs.

Now Scarlett was thoroughly confused. Had Dana decided to do a quick scene with Jane and Gaby up here, before the party started? What about the Jane-Hannah scene?

But Scarlett had no time to stick around and find out. She had to slip in and out of her room and make her escape before Matt or anyone else could stop her. She was on a mission.

30

WHAT HAPPENS IN VEGAS

"The gondola's gonna be here in about ten minutes." Hannah's voice crackled over Jane's earpiece. "I'll make sure the DJ has their song ready."

"Great!" Jane said excitedly. "Everyone's got champagne . . . place looks awesome . . . I think we're ready to start this party!"

Jane signed off and walked briskly across St. Mark's Square, which was actually an indoor version of the world-famous Piazza San Marco in Venice, Italy. She loved the architecture of the shops and restaurants that surrounded the square, with its cream and pastel walls and high, arched windows.

Many of the guests were milling around or sitting at the large round tables decorated with gold silk cloths and antique candelabras. Jane tried to make out who was who, but it wasn't easy, since almost everybody was wearing a costume mask. She knew there were more A-list celebrities than usual because of Aja and Miguel, who were one of the most powerful couples in Hollywood. She spotted D near the VIP seating area, chatting up a model type; she recognized him easily thanks to his purple vintage tux and spiky crew cut. She also saw Veronica Bliss talking to a short dark-haired guy (Jared Walsh?); there was no mistaking the petite redhead in Chanel, mask or no mask. And there were a lot of people *not* wearing masks: Hannah, Oliver, Trevor, Fiona, Xavier and Hank from the Venetian, Aja's assistant, Anna Luisa, her publicist, Wanda, and Gaby's publicist, Annabelle. Although where was Gaby? She must be out there somewhere, along with Caleb, Naveen, Scarlett, and Madison. Not to mention Sophia and Jesse, if they weren't too wasted to make it down from their room.

Jane continued toward the dock where Aja and Miguel would be pulling up momentarily. At the top of the steps leading down to the water was an arch covered with roses, freesias, and tiny white lights. Thousands of flower petals blanketed the steps themselves. Two attendants in ivory waistcoats awaited the couple's arrival. It all looked pretty spectacular, if Jane had to say so herself.

Her phone buzzed with a text; Jane glanced at it quickly and saw that it was from Braden.

FLYING HOME TOM. DINNER MONDAY?

Her heart skipped a beat.
Jane was so tempted to reply YES!!!!! But what about

Caleb? She couldn't be dating Caleb and hanging out with Braden, too—especially since she and Braden were a little more than friends. And also because she had decided to make more of an effort with Caleb. So he was a bit starstruck. Hollywood had that effect on people, and he would get over it soon. In the meantime, he was still the same great guy he always was: fun, sweet, thoughtful. *Hot*. She was going to try to talk him into more off-camera dates so they could be themselves again, the way they used to be, before he got the fame bug and before Dana started micromanaging their conversations. No wonder their on-camera chemistry was so lame, when they couldn't even be themselves most of the time.

"Jane!" Oliver came rushing up to her. "Sorry to bother you, but Fiona wanted me to ask you . . . can we rearrange some seats at the head table? Aja's sister and her husband weren't planning to be here because they live in Martinique and they just had a baby. But they made some last-minute arrangements, and now they're here, and it's supposed to be a big surprise for Aja and Miguel. Is there anything we can do?"

"Ohmigod . . . the head table!" Jane went through a mental picture of the seating chart. Aja, Miguel, Aja's parents, Miguel's parents, Miguel's brother and his wife . . . they couldn't possibly move any of *them* over to another table.

"You know, the tables *are* kind of big," Oliver remarked. "Maybe we could ask Hank or Xavier to have someone squeeze in two more place settings? And maybe get rid of one of the candelabras, to make space?"

"Yes! Oliver, you're brilliant!"

Oliver blushed. "Glad I could help."

"Yeah, well, it would have been a disaster if we couldn't accommodate the sister and brother-in-law."

"Guess I won't be having this problem at *my* celebrity engagement party, since I don't have any siblings," Oliver joked.

Jane smiled. And then her smile faded. Oliver was an only child?

Jane flashed back to another mental picture, of an entry in Trevor's notebook she had never been able to decipher. It was a short entry, with just four items:

Right age, height, attractive
From SD, only child
No acting aspirations, needs $?
Seems very willing to go along with it

Seems very willing to go along with it. Jane felt sick to her stomach all of a sudden as a terrible realization dawned on her.

"Jane? Are you okay?" Oliver sounded concerned.

Jane reached under her clothing and switched her microphone off. She signaled for Oliver to do the same. He obeyed, looking confused.

"Oliver, tell me the truth," Jane said as calmly as she

could. "Did Trevor cast you to date Hannah?"

Oliver stared at her. "W-what are you talking about?" he stammered.

"Did . . . Trevor . . . cast . . . you?"

Oliver started to turn away, then stopped. "Look, it wasn't like that, exactly," he blurted out. "A friend of mine told me that some producer was looking for a guy my age to be on his reality show. I went in for the interview. Trevor practically signed me up on the spot. He said that all I had to do was be a part-time intern for an event planner, and he hinted that I might like some girl named Hannah."

"Nice," Jane said, disgusted.

"It's not what you think!" Oliver said. "I couldn't say no to the money. My dad got laid off last year, and I'm trying to pay my own way through school." He raked a hand through his dark auburn curls. "Besides, you don't understand. Hannah and me . . . it's not like Trevor made me like her. I was just gonna see what happened. But then I fell in love with her."

"You're . . . in love with her?" Jane said, stunned.

"Head over heels. She's the most amazing girl I've ever known."

"Jane!" Hannah's voice came over her earpiece. "The gondola's gonna be here in, like, sixty seconds."

Jane glanced quickly at Oliver. "Oh, hey, Hannah," she said loudly. Oliver looked startled. "I'm on my way. Everything okay where you are?"

"Everything's perfect!"

No, it's not, Jane thought grimly as she signed off, thinking about Oliver's confession. She told herself that Hannah was going to need lots of support in the coming days and weeks. Because she was pretty sure that Hannah was in love with Oliver, too, and it wasn't going to be easy for her when she learned the truth.

Although . . . something told Jane that Hannah would find it in her heart to forgive Oliver. After all, Hannah had done something similar when she first started working for Fiona, pretending to be Jane's friend for the cameras per Trevor's and Dana's instructions.

"Jane, you're not gonna tell her, are you?" Oliver said worriedly. "If she knew Trevor cast me like that, she'll think I'm lying about the way I feel about her. And I'm not!"

Jane put her hands on his shoulders. "No, I'm not gonna tell her. *You* are."

"What?"

"Yep. And it's gonna be okay."

"It is?"

"She might surprise you. She's pretty understanding." Jane gave Oliver a reassuring smile. "Okay, come on, back to work."

Jane switched her mike on and hurried toward the dock, just as the DJ on the stage began playing "At Last" by Etta James. The white-and-gold gondola glided into the square, and the crowd erupted into wild cheers as Aja and Miguel, looking happy and radiant, stood up in the boat, waving and blowing kisses.

"Jane?" A guy in a black tux touched her arm. He lifted his mask.

"Oh, hey, Naveen! Are you having fun? Where's Caleb?" Jane asked him distractedly. She noticed a PopTV camera guy about ten feet away, filming them. *Yeah, Naveen and I are having a pretty fascinating conversation right now,* she thought drily.

"I'm not sure. Have you seen Scarlett?"

"Not in, like, the last half hour. Listen, I'm sorry, but I'm working, so I've gotta run. I'll catch up with you later—*ow!*"

Someone bumped into Jane, hard. She glanced up, startled, and saw a familiar-looking girl holding an empty wineglass.

"I'm such an idiot!" the girl cried out.

Jane looked down and saw the massive red stain blooming across the front of her white silk blouse. "That's okay," she said, trying not to sound as annoyed as she felt. She noticed that the camera guy from before was still filming. *Great.* "I have another blouse in my room. I'll just go up and change."

"Ohmigod, I'm so sorry," the girl apologized.

Jane fake-smiled and hurried to the nearest exit, trying to hide the growing stain with her hand. She spoke briefly to Hannah, letting her know that she would be off-site for a few minutes. She made it to the elevator without receiving *too* many funny looks and pressed 9.

When Jane stepped onto her floor, she made a quick right—and was surprised to see another PopTV camera camped outside her door, along with Matt. The camera guy spotted her and zoomed in on her.

What's going on? Jane wondered. Was her red wine stain emergency really *that* interesting? But she couldn't ask questions during a shoot, so she just kept walking to her door and inserted her key card in the lock.

She was halfway inside the room when she realized that she wasn't alone in there. Two more PopTV camera guys were set up in opposite corners, filming.

And Caleb and Gaby were sitting on the edge of the king-size bed, kissing.

"What? Caleb!" Jane yelled.

Caleb and Gaby jerked apart.

"Janie!" Caleb exclaimed, swiping at the red lipstick smeared on the side of his mouth. "Listen, I can explain. That dude from your show told me to meet you up here so we could do a scene. Then *she* showed up and threw herself at me. I swear!"

"Jane, I'm sorry!" Gaby cried out. "I didn't wanna do this. But Annabelle told me that if I didn't, Trevor was going to kick me off the show!"

"Wait, what?" Caleb said, turning to Gaby.

Jane shook her head and covered her ears. "No! You know what? I'm really not interested in your explanations. Either of you."

"But, Jane!"

"Janie!"

Jane went over to her closet and yanked a fresh white blouse from a hanger. "Have a nice life," she said coldly, and stormed out the door. *So I guess this is what happens in Vegas,* she thought.

Once in the hallway, she pulled out her phone and called up the text from Braden.

DINNER ON MONDAY SOUNDS PERFECT, she typed.

31

SURVIVOR

Madison took a sip of her martini and glanced around St. Mark's Square, wondering what had possessed Jane to suggest a Venetian masked ball. All the people in their feathery black masks were so lame, and the long, flouncy gowns made the girls at the party look old. Madison, on the other hand, had taken care to select the perfect dress for the occasion: a black Prada strapless with an asymmetrical hemline that was at once edgy, stylish, and sexy.

Actually, Madison was supposed to be "on duty" tonight, whatever that meant. But she had no interest; she *attended* parties, she wasn't the help. She hated her event-planning "job" and even pretending to work there for the cameras was getting old. Besides, there was no way she was going to run around the Venetian in a uniform like Jane and Hannah. No wonder Jane's BF had disappeared, and Intern Boy seemed so moody, with their girlfriends looking so frumpy. Madison had half a mind to move in on one or both guys. But what would be the point? She could do better.

Madison's gaze drifted to Aja and Miguel Velasquez slow-dancing out on the floor. Now *there* was a boyfriend worth stealing: a super-hot, super-rich, super-famous baseball player. Her mind reeled with the media possibilities, not to mention the lifestyle upgrades.

"Maddy! There you are!"

Madison turned, sighing. Sophie was staggering toward her, holding a drink with one hand and clinging to Jesse with the other. *Great.* Sophie was halfway to wasted—or possibly already there—and the party had barely begun.

Madison casually switched off her mike and pretended to kiss her sister on the cheek in case anyone was watching. In fact, wasn't that Veronica Bliss talking to the Marley twins? And Veronica's hideous ex-assistant-turned-blogger Diego at the bar?

"For the hundredth time, it's *Madison*, not *Maddy*," she hissed in Sophie's ear. "God, you reek. What is that, pot?"

"You are so old, Maddy!" Sophie whined. "Isn't she old, baby?" She stood on her tiptoes and nibbled on Jesse's neck, looking a little unstable on her five-inch platforms.

Madison caught her by the elbow and steadied her on her feet. She had seen Sophie trashed before, but not quite this bad.

"You wanna hit, Madison?" Jesse whispered, reaching into his breast pocket. "It's good stuff."

"No!" Madison clenched her fists, trying to keep her

voice down. This situation was getting out of control. Aside from the fact that there was press nearby, weren't Sophie and Jesse both miked? It was hard to tell, since Sophie's clingy black halter dress didn't have any telltale bumps underneath, and Jesse was in a tux. Maybe Dana hadn't caught up to them yet?

Madison knew that she had to do something, fast. "Listen, Jesse—can you get us a couple more drinks?" she said sweetly.

Jesse smirked. "Sure, anything for my girls. Be right back."

He lurched toward the bar, bumping into a couple of guests along the way and receiving nasty looks in return. As soon as he was out of earshot, Madison whirled on Sophie. "We're going upstairs."

"Why? I just got here."

"Yeah, well . . . party's over. You're going straight to bed, and we'll talk about this in the morning." Madison put her hand on Sophie's arm and started to steer her toward the exit.

Sophie jerked her arm away. *"What are you doing?"* she screamed. Then she tossed her champagne glass to the ground, shattering it.

The crowd around them stopped talking. Madison froze.

Sophie glared at Madison with glazed, bloodshot eyes. "Who do you think you are, my mother?" she spat out.

"No, Sophie—*Sophia*. But you're in no shape to—"

"Yeah, that's right. *You are not my mother!*" Sophie said, raising her voice as if to make sure everyone could hear. "Cuz Mom lives in a trailer park back East, and you live in a fancy-ass penthouse in Hollywood. Oh, except, it's not even your penthouse. It's your *boyfriend's* penthouse where he keeps you stashed away so his wife doesn't find out. Because you're a whore, Maddy."

Madison felt the blood rushing from her face. Veronica Bliss and Diego and the others were watching and listening intently. Madison heard whispers all around her.

"Sophie, please," Madison said quietly, her desperation rising. "You want money? I'll give you money. I'll give you whatever you want. But just shut up, okay? Or you're gonna ruin everything for both of us."

"God! I'm so sick of you ordering me around!" Sophie shouted. "I'm not your little kid sister anymore. I'm gonna be a *way* bigger star than you ever were. And I don't need to pretend to be someone I'm not to get there. You're so pathetic, faking that you're some rich bitch named Madison Parker just so people will like you. Tell them, Maddy! Tell them your real name . . . Madelyn Wardell!"

There were gasps, then more whispers, then a low, steady rumble of excited chatter all around them. Madison stood there numb with shock, her gaze unfocused, her heart hammering in her chest. She was vaguely aware of a flashbulb popping, and someone calling out her name, and then Sophie muttering, "Shit!" as she grabbed on to a chair and fell.

Good, Madison thought, glancing at her sister passed out on the floor. *Maybe the little bitch is dead.*

Although it didn't matter anymore. Nothing mattered anymore.

Madison's life was over.

Madison leaned against the wall and peered around the dark, enclosed space, wondering where she was—an empty closet? An unused coat-check room? She could hear the muffled sounds of the party in the distance—the DJ was playing Jay-Z—and the rise and fall of conversation and laughter as people passed by in the hall outside.

She had slipped in here on her way upstairs to escape a couple of reporters trying to chase her down for comments. She knew there would be many, many more of them, following her 24/7 and staking out her apartment, as soon as the news had had a chance to spread. In fact, she was already thinking about leaving the country for a while, like Jane did back in December after the *Gossip* story broke.

Except that Madison's screwup was way worse than Jane's. Jane had merely hooked up with her boyfriend's best friend, and lots of girls did crazy stuff like that. Not too many girls faked their identities in order to become famous.

She slumped down to the floor and burst into tears.

"Hey . . . Madison?"

Madison's head jerked up. Blinking in the darkness, she

made out a silhouette in the doorway. Was it a reporter? No, it looked like . . . Jane. *WTF?*

"If you're here to gloat, I'm not interested," Madison snapped, swiping at her eyes angrily.

Jane moved into the room and knelt down next to Madison. Madison saw that she was holding a glass of champagne.

"I saw you come in here," Jane said, handing her the glass. "Thought you could use this."

Madison stared at her in surprise. "You're offering me a drink?"

"Yep."

"But . . . why?"

Jane shrugged. "I don't know. Because you had a really, really bad night?"

Madison frowned suspiciously. "You're not miked, are you?"

"I turned it off. Don't worry, Trevor didn't send me in here. Anyway, that's all. I've gotta get back to work now." Jane rose to her feet.

"Wait! Jane!"

"What?"

"Thank you."

"You're welcome. You'd better check your compact— you've got mascara all over your face, and one of your eyelashes is, like, falling off."

Madison smiled weakly. "Great. My life is ruined, and I look like hell."

"Your life isn't ruined," Jane told her. "You're obviously a survivor, and you'll figure it out. You do look like hell, though. And no, this doesn't mean we're gonna be friends again. But I'm sure I'll be seeing you around." With that, she turned and left.

Madison watched her old friend go. Then she tipped back the glass of champagne, polishing it off, and reached into her clutch for her compact.

Jane was right. Madison *was* a survivor. She would turn this nightmare into an opportunity, somehow. She had always managed to claw her way out of the abyss before. And she would find a way to do it again.

32

HOW AWESOME WAS THAT?

It was almost midnight when Scarlett arrived at Liam's apartment, still wearing her sequined black gown and insanely high heels and dragging her rolling suitcase behind her. She had managed to get the last seat on the 9:35 out of Las Vegas, then caught a cab at LAX, miraculously avoiding paparazzi the whole way.

She knocked, praying he was home. Praying he was home *alone*. Praying he wouldn't want to *be* alone any longer when he saw her there.

Scarlett was about to knock again when the door opened. Liam stood there, wearing only a pair of baby blue pajama bottoms. She tried not to stare. God, she had missed him. It took every ounce of willpower not to throw her arms around him and start kissing him right then and there.

"Scarlett?" He rubbed his eyes. "What are you doing here? And why are you dressed up?"

"I'm sorry, did I wake you? Cuz you usually don't go to bed till later."

"I've got an early shoot tomorrow. My friend Taylor needed an extra camera on a commercial. What's up?"

"Can we talk?"

"Sure. Come on in."

Scarlett followed Liam down the hall and into the living room. "It's just you and me. Ry and Danny are out," he said, sitting down on the couch. "You want something to drink?"

"I'm good, thanks." Scarlett sat down next to him and toyed with her bracelet. She tried to gauge how he felt about her being there; was he happy, relieved, angry, confused, or all of the above? It was hard to tell from his guarded expression.

"Okay, so the reason I'm dressed like this is because I just left Aja's engagement party," she began. "I left before it started, and I didn't even clear it with Dana and Trevor."

"You mean the Venetian hotel shoot? Seriously?"

Scarlett nodded. "I ran to my room and packed my stuff and took a cab to the airport."

"Why the rush?"

"Because I wanted to tell you something." Scarlett paused and gazed into his eyes. "I love you. And I'm so sorry about our fight."

Liam's expression softened. "I love you, too, Scarlett. I really, really love you. And I'm sorry, too." He cradled her face in his hands and kissed her.

Scarlett leaned into the kiss. She was in love with Liam. And he was in love with her. How awesome was that?

But she had to tell him the rest of it. She broke away from the kiss and added, "There's something else."

"Hmm?" Liam caressed her hair.

"I'm leaving L.A."

"Wait, *what*?"

"You know I've never been totally happy at USC, right?" Scarlett explained. "Well, I sent in a bunch of applications in March, to Yale and Columbia and Harvard and a lot of other schools. I wasn't sure I wanted to transfer, but I wanted to keep my options open for this fall. Anyway . . . I got into all of them."

"Seriously?"

Scarlett nodded. "Yeah. So I've been thinking a lot about it, and I've finally made my decision. I want to leave the show. And I definitely want to transfer to one of these schools. I'm just not sure which one yet."

"Wow." Liam looked stunned.

"USC's fine, but you have to understand . . . I never considered going anywhere else because I wanted to live in L.A. with Jane. But I realize now that I can't plan my life around other people. Which is why I have to go." Scarlett laced her fingers through his. "I hope you're okay with this."

Liam was silent for a long moment. Then he nodded slowly.

"I'm totally okay with this," he said finally. "No, not

just okay. I'm really proud of you. You got into some of the best schools in the country. Congratulations!"

Scarlett beamed. "Thanks!"

"And listen, Scarlett . . . I'll support whatever choice you make about school. If you decide to go to Yale or Columbia or wherever . . . well, we'll make it work out."

"Really?"

"Really."

Scarlett wrapped her arms around his neck, and they kissed some more. She had never believed in happy endings, but at that moment, she had one of her very own. She and Liam were in love. She was leaving *L.A. Candy*. And she was going to start a whole new chapter in her life. She wasn't sure where or when or how—but it was definitely going to be amazing.

33

REAL LIFE

The PopTV offices were nearly deserted when Jane walked into the lobby on Monday night. The receptionist was putting on her jacket and packing up her bag, and a cleaning woman was vacuuming noisily in the corner.

"Hey, Maria. Is Trevor still here?" Jane asked the receptionist. She noticed that the flower arrangement on the front desk looked a little wilted.

Maria grinned. "Trevor's *always* here. Go on back, I'll let him know you're coming."

"Thanks."

Jane went through the double doors and headed down the hall. She was surprised at how calm she felt, especially since she had tossed and turned all night, playing this encounter out in her mind over and over. Now, she wasn't nervous at all. In fact, she was almost looking forward to it.

Did this mean she was doing the right thing?

Trevor was waiting in the doorway when Jane reached

his office. "Jane. Good to see you. Come on in."

"Thanks, Trevor."

He sat down and indicated for her to do the same. "Have you eaten? There's a new sushi place around the corner."

"No, thanks. I've already got dinner plans. I just needed to tell you something."

"Of course. What's on your mind?"

Jane reached into her bag, pulled out the brown Smythson notebook, and set it down on Trevor's desk. "I quit," she said simply. "This will be my last season."

"You're not serious." Trevor didn't even glance down at the notebook.

"I'm totally serious."

"Why?"

Jane pointed to the notebook. "This. I'm tired of being a character in your story. I'm tired of having you arrange my life into scenes. And Saturday night? Caleb and Gaby? That was pretty low."

"I didn't *force* your boyfriend to kiss another girl. I can't make anyone do anything they don't want to do. I'm just there to record stuff as it happens."

"Yeah, I'm sure that's what you tell yourself every day."

Trevor frowned. "Look. I get it. I'd be pissed, too. But Caleb wasn't good enough for you, anyway. This frees you up to find another boyfriend, a better boyfriend."

"You mean, it frees me up so *you* can find me a boyfriend? Like you did for Hannah?"

"Jane, I don't know what you're talking about."

"You know exactly what I'm talking about, Trevor. And I'm done."

Trevor leaned back in his chair and stared out the window. The first wisps of pink and purple and yellow streaked the evening sky, and the lights of Los Angeles glittered like jewels. Jane knew he had a lot on his mind already, especially with the big revelation about Madison. "I have to admit, I didn't see this one coming," he said finally. "I knew you had some issues with the show. But quitting?"

"Yeah, well, every once in a while I do something that you didn't write down in your little notebook," Jane said drily.

"Funny. You know that Scarlett wants to leave, too?"

Jane nodded. Scarlett had told Jane her news last night, including the fact that she had decided to transfer to another college in the fall. Talk about mixed emotions; Jane couldn't bear the idea of her best friend leaving L.A., but at the same time, she absolutely wanted Scar to follow her dreams.

"My decision has nothing to do with hers, though," she explained to Trevor. "I have enough reasons of my own. I've been thinking about this for a while—ever since I found your notebook at Coco de Ville."

"My notebook. God, I should burn the damned thing."

"Yeah, you should. But you won't." Jane stood up to go. Trevor stood up, too, and walked over to her. He put his hands on her shoulders and gazed into her eyes. "Jane, you're at the top of your game," he said, his voice full of fatherly concern. "You don't want to quit now. Is it about the money? Because you know that the network will pay you more to stay. It's a bit irregular mid-season, but I can pull some strings. I'll talk to your agent."

Jane met his gaze squarely. "No, it's not about the money. R.J. already knows, and he supports my decision a hundred percent." She added, "Don't worry about the rest of the season. I'll show up for all my shoots, as always, and I'll fulfill my media obligations. After that, well . . ." She paused. "I'm going back to my real life."

"Do you really want to go back to the way things were? Before I discovered you at Les Deux?"

"More than anything," Jane said, meaning it. "Now, if you'll excuse me, I'm late for my dinner date."

Trevor regarded her, his jaw clenching and unclenching. "You're going to change your mind. You know that, right?"

Jane shrugged. And said nothing. She knew Trevor would not give up easily. She also knew there was nothing he could say or do to make her change her mind.

Jane blinked into the morning light and glanced over at her nightstand, expecting to see her goldfish, Penny, demanding breakfast. But instead of her fishbowl, there was a stack of scripts, a Coffee Bean & Tea Leaf travel mug, and a framed, faded photo of a blond boy dressed in a SpongeBob T-shirt and holding a puppy.

Oh, right. Jane rolled over and smiled at Braden, who was curled up on his side, fast asleep. The photo must be Braden at age nine or ten. So cute. She inched closer to him and snuggled against his back. His T-shirt had a warm, beachy smell that she had always associated with him.

She couldn't believe she was here, now, in his bed. They had met for dinner last night at a hole-in-the-wall Thai restaurant (to avoid paparazzi), after which Braden had suggested that they go back to his apartment for a Monopoly rematch, which had turned out to be code for something else, which had been just fine with Jane. As soon as they walked through his front door, they fell into each other's arms and kissed. Their chemistry had been amazing—better than ever. Was it because they had come to realize their true feelings for each other during their time apart?

At dinner, Jane hadn't said a word to Braden about Caleb (whose calls and texts she hadn't returned—and had no plan to return). She hadn't said a word about her conversation with Trevor, either. She was waiting for the perfect moment. Because among other things, quitting the show meant that she and Braden could finally try to have a real relationship. Away from the cameras, away from the spotlight, no more hiding in their apartments or meeting in dive bars and out-of-the-way restaurants. They could date openly, publicly, like a real couple. *Finally.*

"Morning." Braden stretched, then sat up against the

pillows. His dirty blond hair was tousled, and his hazel-green eyes looked sleepy.

"Hey. How are you?"

"Tired. What time did we go to bed?"

"Two or three?"

"God. Sorry. When do you have to be at work?"

"Not till this afternoon. So I'm all yours this morning."

"Cool." Braden kissed Jane on the forehead, then rolled out of bed and headed into the hallway. She heard a door closing, then water running, then a door opening, then footsteps, then a coffee grinder buzzing loudly. *Guess that means we're getting up,* Jane thought. She got to her feet, found her dress lying on the floor, and pulled it on over her camisole.

By the time she walked into the kitchen, Braden was pouring two mugs of coffee. "Do you take anything?" he asked her.

"Just some milk, if you have it." Jane sat down at the small wooden table. "Soooo. I have some news."

"Yeah? What's going on?" Braden set the mugs down on the table and sat across from her. He picked up his BlackBerry and glanced at it briefly.

Jane took a deep breath and began playing with her hair. She tried to anticipate Braden's reaction. Would he be happy? Of course he was going to be happy, right? Even though he had always been 100 percent supportive of her career, he had never held back on his negative opinions about *L.A. Candy*, reality TV, and the whole Hollywood scene. Not to mention the problems these things had caused for the two of them.

"I wanted to tell you last night, but . . . well . . . it's kinda big."

Braden grinned. "What? You're killing me with the suspense."

"Okay. So here it is. I quit the show."

Braden stared at her. "You . . . quit the show?"

"Yep. I told Trevor last night. This is gonna be my last season."

"Wow. What brought *that* on?"

Jane told him about Trevor's notebook and the Caleb-Gaby incident in Las Vegas. "I'm sick of Trevor controlling me," she finished. "I want my life back. I want to be able to do what I want . . . and date who I want."

She paused and glanced at him expectantly.

Braden took a sip of his coffee and looked thoughtful. "Yeah, well, this is huge," he said after a moment. "I'm really proud of you, Jane. That took a lot of guts."

"Thanks!"

"Are you going to quit your other job, too? With, uh, Fiona Chen, right?"

"Right. I definitely want to keep working in event planning. I'm not sure about Fiona's, though. PopTV's pretty much taken over her offices."

"That's nuts." Braden reached for his BlackBerry and started scrolling. "You know, my friend Amanda works at some fancy event-planning firm in New York. I could email her for you, see if they're hiring?"

Jane blinked.

"Yeah, here she is. She works at Four Star Events. Ever heard of them?"

Jane began twisting a lock of her hair around her finger. Did Braden just tell her that he would try to help her find a new job . . . across the country? She had misheard him, right? But he kept on talking . . .

"Amanda Miller. Yeah, I think she really likes it there."

Wait. Had Braden suddenly lost interest in her because she had basically told him she was interested in *him*?

As Braden talked, Jane's mind flashed back to the conversation she had with Scarlett on the ride home from the Playground party. Scar had asked her if Braden was the kind of guy who avoided relationships until he really and truly fell in love—or if he was the kind who avoided relationships altogether. Had Braden ever *been* in a relationship? Jane knew he'd been on-again off-again with Willow for three years, which should have been a warning sign. She also thought about the first time she and Braden hooked up, back in December. Braden had made the overture, not her, and she had been too vulnerable and mixed-up to resist. Should the fact that he came on to her while she was dating his best friend have been a warning sign, too? And what about his late-night phone call from Banff, after he'd heard that she was dating Caleb? Did Braden only want her when she was with another guy, or he was with another girl, or they were otherwise unable to be together?

The answer seemed suddenly obvious.

Here she had been thinking that he might be the one. Not Jesse, not Caleb . . . *Braden*.

God. She was such an idiot.

"Amanda's really cool. I'm sure she'd be happy to talk to you," Braden was saying.

Jane stood up and put her coffee mug in the sink. Then she went to the living room and picked up her shoes and her purse.

"Where are you going?" Braden said, trailing after her. "Are you hungry? We could grab some breakfast."

Jane turned and gazed at Braden. "I've gotta go," she said quietly. "Good-bye, Braden."

Braden frowned. "Wait. What's wrong? What did I do?"

Jane smiled sadly at him. "Nothing. Thanks for last night. But I don't think we're going to be doing that again." She added, "Oh, and let me give you a heads-up. As soon as I walk out that door, you're gonna decide you want me back. You might even tell yourself that you're in love with me. But you're not. You never will be."

With that, she left.

34

BECOMING NOBODIES

"So here's to your amazing new job," Scarlett said, lifting her glass of champagne.

Jane lifted her glass, too. "And here's to your amazing new college. Columbia's not gonna know what hit them," she joked.

"Ha-ha. By the way, Liam and I just ordered a sofa bed for the living room. It's got your name written on it."

"Yeah, well, I'm gonna be sleeping there a *lot*, so don't even bother changing the sheets."

Scarlett giggled. "Ew."

Jane took a sip of her champagne and glanced around the trendy new Rodeo Drive restaurant, checking out the other people there, worried that she might start crying if she didn't distract herself, quick. Outside the window, the air shimmered with the late July heat wave . . . candy-colored convertibles glided by . . . and a row of palm trees swayed slightly in the nearly stagnant breeze. Summer in

L.A. Had it really been a whole year since she and Scar moved here from Santa Barbara?

In a few days, Scarlett and Liam were flying out to New York: Scar for her Columbia University orientation, and Liam to work for a film production company. They had already lined up an apartment in the Morningside Heights neighborhood of Manhattan.

As for Jane, she was going to start her new job next week, with RSVP, a small but high-profile event-planning firm with offices in L.A. and New York. Unlike Fiona, the owner of RSVP had zero interest in being part of a reality show. Jane was really excited about working for him and also having the opportunity to travel to Manhattan for business—and be a total third wheel in Scar's and Liam's lives.

Hannah was coming with Jane to RSVP. She and Oliver had also quit the show and were still together. Jane had dinner with them last week, and was pleased to see how happy they were.

Someday, I'm gonna have what they have . . . and what Scar and Liam have, too, Jane thought. *Someday, I'm gonna find a wonderful guy who loves me for me. Not a Jesse or a Caleb or a Braden, but someone way better.*

In any case . . . *L.A. Candy* was behind her now. Shooting had wrapped in May, and the Season 2 finale had aired in June. Just as Jane had predicted, Trevor had pulled out all the stops to try to get her to change her mind: pleading, cajoling, offering her larger and larger sums of money, and at one point even losing his cool and yelling at her, which was so unlike him. She knew how high the stakes were for him; the show was his baby. He had finally backed off, but she suspected deep down that he was never going to give up. Fine—whatever. Let him keep pleading and cajoling and negotiating and yelling. Jane wasn't interested in coming back, not now, not ever.

Besides, Trevor had his hands full at the moment. In the aftermath of Las Vegas, he had scrambled to rewrite and restructure everyone's story lines. Madison had "left Fiona Chen Events and moved out of the city." In reality, Madison had gone through a brief, intense period of total media humiliation about her sister's revelation in Las Vegas. That was followed by a wave of "Before" and "After" photos that (ironically) ended up impressing a lot of people, landing Madison her own reality show—a makeover show—with one of PopTV's competitors. Even more surprisingly, Madison recently started a charity to give scholarships to underprivileged girls. The Madelyn Wardell Foundation awarded its first scholarship last week to a girl who grew up in the same trailer park as Madison and who wanted to attend USC.

Sophia and Gaby were still under contract, and Jane had heard rumors that they would be the focus of Season 3, starting in September. Sophia had decided to keep the name Sophia Parker (versus Sophilyn Wardell), and Trevor had trumped up some crazy story line about how Sophia had changed her identity in order to escape an abusive boyfriend back home, which had drawn big ratings and a lot of sympathy in the press. Sophia had broken up with Jesse, no surprise, and gone through a string of equally hot, dysfunctional boyfriends in the last couple of months, all of whom would be appearing on future episodes.

Gaby was apparently dating Caleb, which was pretty much too gross for Jane to contemplate. She'd heard through the grapevine that Gaby was having second thoughts about him and about all the other recent changes in her life. She fired her sleazy publicist and went back to wearing her hair, makeup, and clothing the way she used to. Jane wondered how long Trevor would keep her around on the show.

As for Braden . . . well, Jane didn't think about him much anymore. She was surprised at how quickly she had been able to recover and move on. She was obviously stronger than she gave herself credit for. She wasn't the same old Janie Roberts from last summer who didn't know who she was or what she wanted out of life.

She still hadn't figured it out completely. But she was getting there.

The waitress came by with their appetizers. "This is great, I'm starving," Jane said, digging into her cheese plate. Now that she wasn't under a constant media microscope, she wasn't going to worry about gaining an extra pound or two.

"Isn't it so great not to have to wear mike packs anymore?" Scarlett said, popping an olive into her mouth.

"I'm so used to them, I feel practically naked now."

"Right? And not having paparazzi camped outside our building twenty-four/seven?"

"Yeah. It's so lonely without them." Jane laughed, but then got serious again and added, "Speaking of press . . . was Liam okay about your *Maxim* cover?"

"*Wellllll*. He said he was gonna buy every single copy out there and hack the *Maxim* website so no one could see the pictures."

"Yeah, that sounds like Liam. I think Madison's got the September cover?"

"Hmm. Can't wait."

Just then, Jane noticed a guy standing behind a nearby column, looking in their direction. He was middle-aged, balding, and wore a camera strap around his neck. . . .

"Scar! There's a paparazzo inside the restaurant," Jane whispered.

"What? Where?"

Jane nodded in the direction of the column.

"Hey, you!" Scarlett raised her voice. "Yeah, you! We can see you! You'd better get out of here before we call the manager. Paparazzi aren't allowed in this restaurant!"

The man stepped out from behind the column. Jane realized with a start that his camera was not a professional camera. Maybe he was a customer who had been waiting at the bar for his drink?

"*Je ne comprends pas l'anglais,*" he said, looking confused.

"Oh, God, Janie. He's French. He's probably a tourist,"

Scarlett whispered, sounding mortified. "*Je suis désolée!*" she called out, waving. "*Ce n'est rien!* Never mind!" She buried her head in her hands. "Oh, God. How embarrassing was that?"

"Pretty embarrassing. Sorry! I guess I'm still paranoid."

"Yeah, well . . . no one wants to take our pictures anymore. We're practically nobodies now," Scar joked.

Jane grinned and raised her champagne glass. "Here's to becoming nobodies," she toasted.

Scarlett smiled and raised her glass.

ACKNOWLEDGMENTS

Thanks to Max Stubblefield, Nicole Perez, Kristin Putt-kamer, PJ Shapiro, Dave Del Sesto, Adam Divello, Tony DiSanto, Liz Gately, MTV, Zareen Jaffery and Farrin Jacobs and everyone at HarperCollins, Matthew Elblonk, and everyone else who made this book possible.

And a very special thanks to Nancy Ohlin, my collaborator; I've learned so much and have loved creating these books.

Get gossip on the go!

TEXT **CONRAD** TO **READIT** (732348)

U.S. Residents Only / Message and Data Rates May Apply

Or download the 2D bar code reader software from your phone at **http://lacandy.mobi/whatis/.** Then use your phone to snap a photo of this code!

With one click you can watch Lauren's author video, get exclusive makeup tips, and share it all with your friends.

HARPER

An Imprint of HarperCollinsPublishers